The Slopes of War

The Slopes of War

by N. A. Perez

Houghton Mifflin Company
Boston

For information about permission to reproduce selections from this book, write to Permissions,
Houghton Mifflin Harcourt Publishing Company, 215 Park Avenue South, New York, New York 10003.

www.hmhco.com

The author was greatly assisted by the National Park Service's superb facilities
at Gettysburg, Pennsylvania, and by the Adams County Historical Association.

Library of Congress Cataloging-in-Publication Data

Perez, Norah H.
The slopes of war.
Summary: Buck Summerhill, a young soldier from Gettysburg, Pennsylvania,
faces the horrors of the Battle of Gettysburg knowing that his
two cousins, Custis and Mason, may be fighting against
him in the Army of Northern Virginia.
PA ISBN-13: 978-0-547-01614-6
1. Gettysburg, Battle of, 1863—Juvenile fiction. 2. United States—History—Civil
War, 1861–1865—Juvenile fiction [1. Gettysburg, Battle of, 1863—Fiction.
2. United States—History—Civil War, 1861–1865—Fiction] I. Title

PZ7.P426S1 1984   83-26436
[Fic]

Printed in the United States of America

DOC 10 9 8 7

4500523991

To Lou,
who walked with me

Contents

Officers and Men of the Army of the Potomac (Union Army)

Colonel Hiram Berdan   *Commander First U.S. Sharpshooters*
General John Buford   *Commander First Division U.S. Cavalry*
General Ambrose E. Burnside
General S. S. Carroll
Colonel Joshua L. Chamberlain
Lieutenant Alonzo H. Cushing
Private George Dawson*
Private Jesse Flynn*
Sergeant Fred Fuger
General Ulysses S. Grant
General Winfield Scott Hancock   *Commander of Second Corps*
Corporal Alphonse Hodge
General Joseph Hooker   *Relieved of command of Union Army three days before Battle of Gettysburg*
General Oliver O. Howard   *Commander of Eleventh Corps*
Reverend Horatio S. Howell   *Union chaplain*
General Henry Hunt   *Chief of Artillery*
General George B. McClellan   (*Little Mac*) *Twice relieved of command of Union Army*
General George Gordon Meade   *Commander of Army of the Potomac*
Captain Walter G. Morrill
Private Charles Payne*
General John F. Reynolds   *Commander of First Corps*
General John Sedgwick   *Commander of Sixth Corps*
General Daniel E. Sickles   *Commander of Third Corps*
Corporal Johnston Skelly   (*Jack*)

General Henry Slocum
Artilleryman Chauncy Sullivan*
Private Buck Summerhill*
General George Sykes   *Commander of Fifth Corps*
Colonel Strong Vincent
Captain Adam Waite*
General G. K. Warren   *Chief of Army Engineers*
General Stephen Weed
Private Tully Willard*

* Fictional characters

Officers and Men of the Army of Northern Virginia
(Confederate Army)

Colonel E. P. Alexander   *Chief of Artillery during Battle of Gettysburg*

General James J. Archer

General Lewis Armistead

Private Wesley Culp

General Jubal Early

General Richard S. Ewell   *Commander of Second Corps*

General R. B. Garnett

General Henry Heth

General A. P. Hill   *Commander of Third Corps*

General John B. Hood

General Thomas J. Jackson   *("Stonewall") Former commander of Second Corps*

General Edward Johnson

General J. L. Kemper

General Robert E. Lee   *Commander of the Army of Northern Virginia*

General James Longstreet   *(Old Pete) Commander of First Corps*

General Lafayette McLaws

General Dorsey Pender

General Johnston J. Pettigrew

General George E. Pickett   *Division Commander (First Corps) Led* "Pickett's Charge"

General Robert E. Rodes

General J. E. B. Stuart   *(Jeb) Commander of Cavalry Division*

Major Walter Taylor *Aide to General Lee*
General Isaac R. Trimble
Private Custis Walker*
General James A. Walker
Private Mason Walker*
General A. R. Wright

* Fictional characters

Cast of Characters

People of Gettysburg

Aunt Beckie
John L. Burns
Mrs. Burns
Henry Culp
Colonel Fahnestock
Dr. Robert Horner
Dr. David Kendlehart
Georgia McClellan
Charles McCurdy and family
Mary Elizabeth Montfort and family
Tillie Pierce and family
Owen Robinson
Shriver family
Snyder family
Leander Summerhill*
Lydia Summerhill*
Rebekah Summerhill*
Mary Virginia (Jennie) Wade
Weikert family
David Wills
Philip (Petey) Winters

Others

Edward Everett
Abraham Lincoln
Aunt Mercy Walker*

* Fictional characters

Before

1

"HURRY! HURRY UP, BOYS — HURRY ALONG!"

Buck knew that he would feel better as soon as he crossed over into Pennsylvania. For days now the Union army had marched through rain and mud and searing sunshine, goaded on by the officers, ordered to hurry, always to hurry. The men were hungry, thirsty, exhausted. Hundreds, maybe thousands, had straggled behind or dropped by the roadside in the appalling heat. Some had tried stuffing leaves inside their caps or cutting green boughs to shade their heads and ward off stroke, but many had died, and it was a sure thing more would fall.

Buck touched the shoulder of the soldier moving ahead of him along the dusty turnpike. "Tully? We're getting close to home."

Tully didn't answer. His head listed forward, shoulders bent under fifty pounds of equipment, boots moving heavily, steadily in a mechanical route step. He might have been asleep on his feet. It was possible to do it, Buck knew, at least until some loud shouted command kicked a dreaming soldier back into his senses. "Close up, boys! Close up!"

3

Always that urgency to push on.

As the long soiled blue columns pushed up through Maryland, spanked northward by the regimental bands, Buck could only guess where the Army of the Potomac was headed. Somewhere on the far side of the Blue Ridge Mountains he knew that another army was snaking forward through hot rising dust, and that when the two forces collided there was going to be a desperate encounter. Maybe this time it would be a fight to the finish.

Ahead the band broke off abruptly in the middle of "The Girl I Left Behind Me." Around a bend in the road an orchard had appeared, green trees sparkling with ripe fruit. Musicians were running toward it, followed by a crowd of cheering soldiers, while officers on horseback plunged up and down among the broken ranks trying to restore order.

"Cherries, Tull! Come on — let's get some!"

Tully stood motionless in the road, swaying under the weight of the heavy pack, his cap, pants, and woollen jacket soaked with sweat.

Buck asked, "What's the matter?"

Tully said vaguely, his torn lips cracked with heat, "Been thinking, I guess. About that hand."

The skeleton hand again. Tully had fretted over it ever since that incident a few days before when the division had rested at the old Bull Run battlefield.

"Forget it, Tull. You're not going to get spooked by some old bones, are you?" Manassas the rebels called that eerie and depressing place where they had licked the Union army twice. It was scarred, ravaged ground, still littered with old rusted muskets and discarded cartridge boxes and rotted knapsacks. Buck remembered how his friend, sprawled beside a pungent clump of pennyroyal, had leaped to his feet as if he'd been stung.

"What is it?" Buck had asked.

And Tully had silently indicated where, among the ragged weeds, a long, delicate wasted hand was pointing at him. Over the past year wind and weather had scattered the fragile covering of many of the shallow graves, and Buck had noticed exposed skulls and ribs and whitened pelvises. So why did Tully have to take one grisly skeleton hand as some kind of sinister omen that he couldn't shake out of his head? No matter that Buck had reasoned as firmly and kindly as he could that a few random bones didn't mean a thing.

"Now don't go getting fixed notions about it. We've seen fellows make premonitions come true, haven't we?" He mentioned the tentmate on the Peninsula who, before a battle, had handed over farewell letters to his folks, with his testament and burial instructions. "And he didn't come back, did he? We buried him because *he* had decided it was all over for him." Then there was the comrade, always joking and whistling, who had become strangely quiet before another fight and had written his name and the date of his death on a bit of paper and pinned it to his shirt. "I guess we knew he wasn't coming back,

5

either." It was their own superstitious fear, Buck explained, that had killed both of them. But Tully wouldn't be reasoned with. He'd been odd ever since Fredericksburg, when he had lain beneath stiff stacked bodies for thirty hours, with nothing to eat or drink, not even able to raise his head without that dead, peculiar thunk of minie balls striking the frozen flesh around him. That was in December. Ever since then he'd gradually slumped deeper inside himself.

Men had been rounded up from the orchard and were being prodded back onto the road again. Gaily the musicians picked up the girl they had left behind right in the place where they had dropped her.

"Close up — close up." The order rang along the sagging columns as hundreds of weary feet pounded *hurry, hurry, hurry, hurry* along the turnpike.

"I wonder where Custis and Mason are, Tull." Buck had two cousins in the rebel army. He talked a lot, trying to force his friend to stay alert and on the surface as they shuffled forward. He glanced toward the hazy mountains to the west where he knew the supple leather whip of the Army of Northern Virginia was cracking northward. "Do you suppose any of those fellows over there know that we're after them?"

"Course they do." It was Jesse Flynn close behind. "That cavalry officer Stuart . . . why, he tells Bobby Lee every time one of us takes a squat in the bushes."

Buck didn't like Jesse much. He had developed a

6

taste for commissary whiskey and playing bluff and even chewing tobacco under his guidance, and he knew how hurt and disappointed his mother would be if she knew how low he had sunk. Tully had nothing to do with Flynn, and he was still as chaste as the day he had enlisted.

Across the mountains the Army of Northern Virginia moved swiftly. Necessity, early in the war, had taught it how to travel fast and light. Between sixty and seventy thousand men, with frayed blankets wrapped around lean bodies, climbed upward into Pennsylvania; many of them were without boots, their cracked feet raw and bleeding from the march. These soldiers were used to scarcity and hardship and doing without, but they had pride and confidence in themselves, in their cause, and in their superb leadership. Down south they had shown that one skinny rebel was worth a dozen Yankees, and they intended to prove it again, this time on northern soil.

Private Jesse Flynn was wrong. General Jeb Stuart, the most famous cavalryman in the country, who twice before in the war had romped around the Union army and never been touched, hadn't reported anything yet to his commander. Ordered to protect the right flank of the Southern forces, Stuart had decided to ride clear around the enemy and cross the Potomac east of the Blue Ridge Mountains before striking north. Unexpected problems had come up, and he had been forced to make a wide detour. Now, in the last burning week of June, Stuart was cut off, completely out of touch with the long gray line of moving men.

And General Robert E. Lee did not have the least idea of the whereabouts of the Union army.

2

"MOTHER? MOTHER, THEY'RE COMING! THEY REALLY are coming!"

The front door banged open. Bekah, who had run all the way from the Ladies' Seminary, stood gasping in the hallway, her cheeks almost the same hot auburn as her flying hair.

"Who's coming?"

"Rebs, Mother! Rebs!"

A woman's voice said from the kitchen, "I'll believe that when I see it."

"But it's true! They're riding into town right now!"

Lydia Summerhill, who had been browning coffee beans at the kitchen range, set aside the flat-bottomed pan and hurried toward the front of the house. "You've seen them?"

"Hundreds! Grinning and shouting, and not two

dressed alike. Some of them *smiled* at me, and waved their hats." Bekah was sputtering, indignant. "Oh, the nerve of them!" There was a rising clatter in the street, a sudden spattering of gunfire. "Here they are now — take a look for yourself!"

Whooping closer and closer came a high, shrill, jubilant yell, and moments later a dusty man on horseback rode down Baltimore Street in the bright sunshine, followed by more and more cavalrymen. After an anxious month of rumors and reports, and at least a dozen false alarms, the enemy was here at last; yet to Bekah the men looked more like tattered scarecrows than dangerous young soldiers.

Again the eerie, high-pitched scream shivered in the air. Mrs. Summerhill slammed the door shut and fiercely bolted it. "Now there'll be a fight!"

"Here?" Everyone had known a big battle was coming, but when Lee had invaded Pennsylvania, Bekah had thought it was Harrisburg or Baltimore or Washington he threatened, not a little market town like Gettysburg.

"Surely not here, but somewhere — and soon! And wherever it is, it's likely Buck will be in it." Mrs. Summerhill was getting worked up, her nose burning red at the tip. "Oh my nerves . . . my poor nerves."

Bekah was not fond of her mother's nerves. They had arrived shortly after Mr. Summerhill died, and like fussy tenants were easily disturbed. Weather bothered them, and excitement of any kind, and the war news most of all. She said, "Don't get yourself all upset."

"But we're here alone — two unprotected females!"

"And Leander."

"He's only a boy, Rebekah."

"I'm not scared."

"That's because you've never had the sense to be afraid."

It hurt, but the girl held her tongue. That was the difference between the two of them. Her mother worried constantly that something might happen to them, while Bekah was sure that nothing ever would. She headed for the kitchen. "I'll make you some tea."

Mrs. Summerhill followed her down the hall. "You're a good girl, and I'm sorry I'm being so foolish. It's just my poor nerves. . . . I'd better take something to calm me down."

It bothered Bekah that her mother soothed herself so often with a dose of laudanum. Better, she thought, to get rid of those nerves for good. Buck could have reasoned with her, in that slow, easy, thoughtful way of his, but Buck had been gone since the spring of '61. He and Tully Willard had been working in a foundry in Erie when the call came for volunteers, and both of them had enlisted in the 83rd Pennsylvanians.

The war had been Buck's great adventure then. He had enjoyed the rough camp life, even the marching and drilling, and looked forward to military action, *seeing the elephant* he called it, before the rebels were whipped, and scolded back into the Union. Two years later his letters had changed. He was concerned about his friend, for one thing.

> Tully isn't the same, and I must confess that I believe his mind is sick. I made him go and see the surgeon, but the man said there was nothing to be done, and gave him the same pills he gives to everyone for every sort of ailment. I just think that if I could get Tully home, so he could rest his thoughts from all the hard things he has seen, it might help him some.

The last note had been brief. It was as if Buck were looking wistfully over his shoulder at his growing up days. He remembered picnics at Ziegler's Grove, and shooting squirrels up on Cemetery Hill. He said he missed cold milk, sweet corn, fresh gingerbread. He mentioned his cousins Custis and Mason Walker, who had enlisted in the Southern army.

> I think of them a lot these days and wonder if they are still alive. I worry most about Mason — remember how he liked to stay in the house and read and play the piano all the time? How would he ever manage in the army? Custis will always get by, I think. Do you recall the summer when he came to visit, and the night the three of us stayed up on Little Round Top talking, and looking at the falling stars, you and Custis and me? He thinks a lot of you, Bekah. Now I must go as we are packing up to leave here in a big hurry. Nobody has told us where we are going, but I wish we were heading home. Will you pass along my fond regards to Mary Virginia?
>
> In haste,
> Buck

11

Her brother could be close to Gettysburg. Custis and Mason, too. The animal war that had prowled across the southland, whose tail lashed Vicksburg, had stretched across Mason and Dixon's line to curl its claws into the frightened North. Now, with the arrival of the enemy forces, Bekah was keyed-up, curious, excited, and angry, but she wasn't at all afraid.

3

TWELVE-YEAR-OLD LEANDER SUMMERHILL AND HIS best friend Charles McCurdy stood in the schoolyard discussing the Fourth of July. The holiday, just eight days away, wouldn't be any fun without a spectacular explosion, yet neither of them had any money to buy powder.

"Maybe the Fahnestocks will give you some chores to do at the warehouse." Charles was always good at thinking up jobs for Leander.

"I've already asked. They've packed up their goods and sent them off to Philadelphia so the rebs won't get them." Most of the other merchants in town had done the same thing. Even the bank had sent away its cash. Leander thought of something else. "How about your grandmother? Grandmothers always have jobs that need doing."

"But not for pay. Just for cookies and stuff." Charles laughed. "Mine made me bury her best silver spoons in the garden. As if the rebels planned on a tea party when they came to town!"

Leander thought this was a great joke. Invasion rumors had kept Gettysburg in a state of anxiety for weeks, with people leaving and coming back, and stashing money and valuables out of sight, and then digging them up again. Days ago the colored people, even those who were freeborn, had packed their belongings and gone for good, taking no chances that they'd be captured and sent south into slavery. Owen Robinson, the sexton of the Presbyterian church, had gone with them, leaving his two pigs with Mr. McCurdy for safekeeping. Charles had the job of feeding them.

He confided to Leander, "I stowed my box of things up in the rafters. Those rebs would go crazy if they saw that slingshot of mine. . . . I reckon there'd be a big fight for it."

Leander was sure of it. His own treasures, bits of glass and iron, nails and screws, and his prize marbles were safely hidden under his mattress.

A shout went up that the rebels were coming. Charles and Leander didn't believe it. They knew all about war, having read Abbot's *Life of Napoleon* and *Scott's Campaigns in Mexico*. They had hoped to see some of its spectacle and glamour splash through the staid streets of Gettysburg, but after so many false alarms they had almost given up. Yet there was a distant popping that might have been a pistol shot, followed by another.

"Come on!" Leander was running. "Even if it's not the war it might be a murder or something!"

A crowd of old men and young boys had collected out on the Chambersburg Pike where they stood in a light rain staring off in the direction of the gunfire. John Burns, an old Scot who had fought in the War of 1812, danced in a circle, punching his thin arms in the air, warming up. "If they've come for a fight, I'll give them a fight!"

"You show 'em, John!" a man yelled.

Leander grinned at the idea of the tiny five-foot constable taking on the rebel army with those little, hard bare fists. Horses appeared over the crest of the hill, pounding closer, and he felt a thumping commotion in his chest as a procession of cavalry streaked past — dirty, scrawny men on starved-looking horses, a confusion of flapping faded rags and whirling hats and wailing war whoops. There was something almost playful in the way the soldiers yelled and fired their revolvers, and Leander wondered if their hearts were really in it. He knew he ought to run for home, that his mother and his sister were alone, and that he was supposed to be the man of the house, but the invasion didn't look so dangerous after all, and he didn't want to miss a minute of it. With Charles he joined the mob of boys racing after the horses down the turnpike.

By the time he reached the town square, called the Diamond, the men were milling around the flagpole where the Stars and Stripes hung limply in the warm June drizzle. Others were spreading out along the empty streets, banging on locked doors, peering with shaded eyes into shop windows.

"Who'll get me bread and butter?" It was a ragged trooper, holding out a fistful of bills. "I'll pay."

A boy spoke up. "That's Confederate scrip. Ain't no good here."

"Please." The officer had a gaunt face, brown from the sun, and worried eyes. "I haven't eaten anything today."

It made Leander feel uncomfortable to know that the man was hungry, when he had never missed a meal in his life. He moved toward the noisy uproar down the street. Some of the rebels had found Petey Winters hiding in the apartment back of his cake and candy store, and forced him to open the shop. Soldiers were crowding in, scooping up peppermint and fudge and ginger cakes. The trooper who had asked for bread and butter came out with his hat full of molasses taffy, and began to pass it around among the town boys. Leander felt ashamed, but he took a piece anyway.

"You wouldn't know my cousin Custis Walker, would you?" Custis was long and lanky and likeable, and would be sure to be well-known in the Southern army. Mason was frail and played the piano, and Leander didn't mention him.

"Who's he with?"

"Stonewall Jackson's brigade, sir."

"Jackson's dead. . . . You know that, don't you?"

"Yes, sir. I read the papers."

"Well, I don't know your cousin. General Ewell's in charge of the Corps now . . . you might catch sight of him. Baldheaded fellow . . . beaky nose and a wooden leg . . . keep your eyes open." The trooper climbed back on his horse, glancing around the square at the civilians peeking out from the alleys and from around the corners of the buildings. He frowned. "How come there are so many able-bodied men left in town? Won't they fight?"

The sun was shining through the rain as Leander squinted up at him. "I guess our army has all it needs right now, but lots have gone. My brother Buck and Tully Willard and Mr. Montfort and Billy Weikert, and a whole lot more."

The trooper's eyes were tired. He twisted the shaggy end of his moustache, half-smiling. "All the men in the North won't be much use to a bad general like Pop Hooker. Why, in May we made him pop out of the wilderness like a parched pea!"

Infantry was marching into the Diamond, shuffling men in faded gray- and butternut-colored uniforms, with a band in the lead piping "The Bonnie Blue Flag."

"What did he say?" Charles shouted over the music, as the trooper rode slowly away down the street.

Leander shrugged. He didn't feel like repeating it.

16

4

"NO, SIR!" DR. KENDLEHART SAID ABSOLUTELY,
when General Early demanded flour, whiskey, pork,
bacon, sugar, coffee, salt, onions, five hundred hats,
and a thousand pairs of shoes, or ten thousand dollars
in cash. "Stores will be open, and the citizens will
give you what they can, but I can't promise any more
than that."

And so on Saturday morning, June 27, the rebels
had left town, with full stomachs but empty hands.
Everyone was proud of the president of the borough
council for speaking up that way, but Bekah did feel
a pang about the shoes. Even though she hated the
sight of the soldiers, it had bothered her to see so
many barefooted men. She had given an old, broken
pair of Buck's boots to a polite young soldier who had
come to the door and asked for something to eat.
He'd been delighted to get them and had enjoyed
Mrs. Summerhill's freshly baked bread and home-
made apple butter, too. When he left he had said
wistfully, "You-uns sure have a heap of truck and
fixin's here." Bekah couldn't forget the words or his
thin lonesome face. Others came after him. The
Summerhills gave what they had, biscuits and pre-
serves and a baked ham pared down to the bone.
There hadn't been much left for supper, but none of

them had complained — not even Leander, who, according to his mother, had a hollow leg.

"It could have been Buck among strangers," she said, "looking for something to stick to his ribs. I only hope some Southern lady would do the same for our boys. I know your Aunt Mercy would."

"You miss her, don't you?" Bekah asked. Ever since the early days of the war there had been almost no communication with her aunt, except for a few messages smuggled back and forth by friends in Baltimore.

"She's my own flesh and blood, and I'll always love Mercy and your cousins no matter what side of the war they live on!"

It was strange that Custis and Mason might be nearby with the Army of Northern Virginia. That night, when Bekah saw the campfires sparkling eight miles west of town, she wondered if the Walker boys might be looking at the shining gas lamps of Gettysburg thinking of their relatives. No matter how angry she was with the South over the rebellion, she could never think of those two as her enemies.

But it was Custis who was special to her. He had been fifteen when she had last seen him in the summer of 1860. There was a bond, a special flow of feelings, between the two of them. She could run as fast, throw as far, climb as high, do anything that Custis dared to do, and what one couldn't think up, the other would. Leander had been peeved and jealous the whole time Custis stayed with them, because he couldn't keep up while the other three roamed everywhere together. Buck was the serious one, and when the wild laughter of the other two was too much for him, he would slip off by himself. He was in love with Mary Virginia Wade that year, but she was older and hardly seemed to notice him. Sometimes he brooded. She was so beautiful to him with her high shining crown of braided hair, and she seemed so out of reach to a boy of sixteen.

When Custis went back to Shepardstown, he had written to Bekah, frank, funny letters that showed another side of him, a gentle and romantic side that she had only guessed was there. Soon she realized that he was the one person in the world that she could tell her heart to, that nothing about herself could shock him or change his feelings for her. Not even her best friend, Tillie Pierce, knew her as completely as Custis did. Then the war came the following spring, and one of the worst things about it was not getting letters from him anymore, and not being able to share her most intimate thoughts and emotions with the person who understood her best.

Over the weekend the rebels burned bridges and twisted the railroad tracks outside of town before moving on to York, where they took twenty-eight thousand dollars in cash from the residents.

"Now I don't feel quite so sorry about them being hungry and barefoot!" Bekah told her mother indignantly. Rumors chased back and forth all over Gettysburg. Most of the government officials, afraid they might be captured and sent down south to the terrible Libby Prison, had already locked their offices and houses and gone away. More and more citizens were also packing their belongings, shutting up their homes and leaving for safer places. All during June, farmers in the area had been sending off their stock across the Susquehanna, and anyone who still owned an animal was looking for a place to hide it. Charles felt a special responsibility for Owen Robinson's prize pigs.

"What will I do with them if the rebels come back?" he asked Charles. "I can't hide *them* up in the rafters!"

"How about under your bed?"

"Why not?" Charles grinned. "My mother always says that my room looks like a pigsty!"

So much was going on. A neighbor developed painful gout in his big toe and blamed it on the invasion, and soon Dr. Horner was treating all sorts of rebel-related diseases, everything from diarrhea to dyspepsia. A few doors away on Baltimore Street young Mrs. McClellan gave birth to a fine healthy child, but she didn't blame it on anyone but Mr. McClellan, who was off with the Union army. Her sister, Mary Virginia Wade, came to lend a hand with the new baby, and when Mrs. Summerhill stopped by she came back with more upsetting news.

"Poor Jennie" — it was her pet name for Mary Virginia — "she thinks her sweetheart was in that last bad fight at Winchester, and she hasn't had a word from him since."

"He'll be all right." Bekah had known Jack Skelly

all her life. He was too vital and full of life to ever have anything serious happen to him. Besides, he and Jennie were to be married soon; nothing could happen now to spoil their plans.

"I know how anxious Jenny must be. . . . These are nervous times for everyone." Mrs. Summerhill took the laudanum bottle from the shelf, her hands trembling as she removed the cork. "Sometimes I can't help wondering what this dreadful war is all about."

"The South wanted independence, and it started this fight, and now we have to finish it!"

"Yes, and I want it to end the way Mr. Lincoln wants it to end, with the country whole again, and not broken into two bitter pieces. But as to who is right or who is wrong . . . what the people in the South want is to govern their own states as they see fit, and preserve their own way of life. Is that really so terrible? Couldn't we have worked something out?"

It confused Bekah when her mother peered around the corners of things, trying to see the other side. As far as Bekah was concerned there was only one side to this war. "But we're in the right!" she insisted. "Because their way of life means owning other people, and living off their labor, and that's a sin!"

"But that was changing. Eventually slavery would have been abolished. . . ."

"If I were being sold at an auction, I wouldn't give a pin about eventually," Bekah said. "And I hate the rebels for firing on our flag, and making our men go into the army, and spoiling our lives. I hate them!"

"Hating's easy." Mrs. Summerhill swallowed a

21

spoonful of medicine, giving the little shiver she always did as it went down. "What's hard is sitting down and trying to work things out, to understand another point of view, to be fair. And when I think about that poor ragged army we saw, and those poor pitiful *children* that we fed . . . then it still seems wrong to me . . . a horrible mistake."

"Mother, you just don't understand." Bekah wanted to believe the politicians and the black and white newspaper editorials that made all the complex issues simple. Yet something her mother had said was true. The easiest thing about the war was hating rebels. The hardest was waiting to see what would happen next.

5

SITTING ON THE PORCH OF A NEAT WOODEN FARM-house south of Chambersburg, a fat boy with a straw hat full of cherries squinted hard against the sunlight as men on horseback halted in the road.

They had come. Too late now to run and warn his father in the fields. But the horses and cattle were already hidden; there was nothing else that he could do. The boy watched as two riders detached themselves from the others, and came slowly along the lane leading to the house. The younger officer, neatly uniformed, dismounted and came briskly across the sunbaked yard. "Could we please get some water, son?"

Water? Surely his father wouldn't object to that. But the boy was unable to move or stop staring in fascination at the other older man, handsome and bearded, seated high upon his graceful horse.

"The pump," the officer persisted. "If you'd kindly show me where it is."

The boy spat a cherry pit and moved toward the back of the house, hurrying now, hoping that his father wouldn't suddenly appear and start an argument. His father didn't care who won the war, as he often said in his slow, heavy accent; he had come to this country to live in peace. All he cared about was making money, and the boy knew that if he could squeeze a profit from these gentlemanly soldiers he would do it.

The tall, gray man on the tall, gray horse was worried. He had moved his sinewy forces into Pennsylvania hoping to draw the Federal army out into the open where he could destroy it on Northern soil. A victory here would force recognition of the Southern Confederacy and end the conflict. Everyone was sick of the war, and no one more so than he, sick of death and mutilation, hunger and dysentery, upheaval and hatred. Now, with a peace movement swelling in the North, was the right time. Still, he was deeply worried.

His eyes moved across the rich landscape, taking in the broad slope of the red barn, a bright haze of ripening grain, the satin sweep of cornfields fiercely green. He was still amazed by the fullness and abundance. His loved Virginia was a dead land now, stripped and burned and blighted after two dreadful years. Let the North feed his hungry army, then, and the animals it needed to keep moving. He had ordered his troops not to bother the citizens and to pay them for whatever they had to take. Pushing into enemy territory was a risky thing to do, but he was used to risk, and to taking chances. He had the will and the nerve to seize the offensive, to win.

"General Lee. . . ."

"Thank you, Taylor."

His aide passed him a cold metal dipper, drops of water spilling silver in the sunlight. As the man on the horse drank and drank the solemn boy was startled from his shyness, knowing now who the tall rider was.

"You're General Lee?"

From a great height dark eyes looked down on him kindly. A smile. A nod.

Even more daring, the boy asked, "Is Jeb Stuart with you?" Everyone knew about General Stuart, with his cocky plumed hat, his love of music, and his way of saying, "Come, boys," instead of "Go, boys."

24

If he were anywhere nearby the boy didn't want to miss a chance of seeing him.

"No, he's not."

"Then, where is he?"

And the commander, sitting upright and dignified upon the splendid horse, said quietly, "I wish I knew, son. I wish I knew."

Skeins of men had been loosely unraveled across the state of Pennsylvania and now, on urgent orders, they were being drawn together, the separate strands being pulled in from the Blue Ridge Mountains and York and Carlisle and Chambersburg to where the roads made a knot at Gettysburg. A Confederate spy had finally told Lee what he should have known much earlier. The Union army was on the move and dangerously near.

"Stand up, son." It amused Custis Mayhew Walker, who had the longest legs in Company B, Second Virginia, that his small friend, Wesley Culp, who had the shortest, was able to keep up in the Stonewall Brigade, one of the fastest units in the army. "How come you insist on marching on your knees like that? Don't you know it looks undignified?"

"Go ahead. Have your fun. But if you keep picking on me I'll tell my sisters on you when we get to Gettysburg."

Private Culp, twenty-four years old and heavily bearded, was used to his eighteen-year-old companion, still without a whisker on his face, calling him son and joking about his size and making fun of his special made-to-order gun.

"You really think that's where we're going, Wes?"

"I sure hope so."

Wes was a Yankee, born in Pennsylvania. He'd moved to Virginia when his employer had moved his carriage business to Shepardstown a few years before, and he'd liked it and stayed. When the war had come along he'd volunteered to fight on the side of the Confederacy.

Custis, swinging easily along the pike, peered down from his height of six foot two. A worn blanket was looped around his thin frame, and he had a toothbrush stuck jauntily in the pocket of his faded shirt. Long, sunstreaked hair flowed out from under the brim of his soft hat. "I have relatives in Gettysburg, you know."

"I know. The Summerhills. I remember Buck and Leander, and that girl with all the wild red hair."

"Bekah." Custis grinned, the memory of her smiling in his bright blue eyes.

Wes, dust smoking up from under his feet, said, "I used to think that Gettysburg was the center of the whole world once. It seemed to me that all the roads went there. And then one day it was as if they turned and went the other way. And so did I."

"Guess you never thought you might end up fighting in your own backyard."

"Still don't seem likely. Nothing ever happens in that sleepy little place. Why do you think I left?"

"You heard our Southern belles were prettier." Custis made a sunbonnet out of his floppy hat, flirted his lashes, and dropped a curtsy, and Wes Culp laughed. He was hot and tired and hungry, but Custis could always make him laugh.

"Don't you feel strange, though," Custis asked, "being so close to your old hometown, but standing on the wrong side of the fence, so to speak?"

Wes took a long, satisfying swallow from his cedar canteen. "Home is where I live now, and that's Virginia. And as far as I'm concerned, it's the right side of the fence. This war isn't where you were born, Cus . . . it's how you feel about things. And I don't believe people in Washington should tell us how to live. Why don't Lincoln and the big fellows leave us alone? That's all we're asking, ain't it? Just to be left alone?"

Custis agreed. "Live and let live, Wes . . . that's how I see it, too. People here don't understand our kind. They think we're all down there flogging slaves. Well, I don't own one, and neither do you. In fact, we don't know anyone who does. But those who do probably take care of them just fine. What they don't catch on to up here is that colored people are like little helpless children. They're really happier and better off when other folk take care of them." He and Bekah had argued about it once, and she had called his notions *archaic.* That was Bekah, trying to win an argument by hitting him over the head with a whole lot of heavy words. *Antediluvian* and *abomination* were two more of her favorite weapons.

Wes said, "My sisters can't understand it, either.

27

Or my brother Will, or the friends I grew up with like poor Jack Skelly."

"Was he that fellow you ran into back at Winchester?"

Wes nodded. "I'm worried about him, Cus. Jack's hurt real bad, and I don't know what will happen to him when he's sent down South to prison. You know we don't have food or medicine for those fellows. We treat them just as bad down there as the Yankees treat the Southern boys in the hellholes up here." He took another swig of water from his canteen. "It sure was a shock seeing Jack poked along the road like that looking so sick. He gave me a letter to give to his girl in case we passed through Gettysburg. I doubt if she'll ever see him again."

It excited Custis to think that they might soon reach the place that meant so much to him, the place where Bekah was. But that girl had powerful feelings. What if she hated the sight of him in his Confederate uniform? His long legs stretched farther, moved faster. Once they had been able to talk about anything, but how could he explain to her how proud he was to be in the Stonewall Brigade, celebrated in the army for its amazing tactical speed? In May, at Chancellorsville, it had pulled off another dazzling maneuver when it had routed the Eleventh Corps and demoralized the whole Union force, but he couldn't very well brag to her about that. It had been a bitter victory, anyway. Stonewall had been wounded by his own men in a queer, unfocused twilight when he had been mistaken for an enemy soldier. His arm had been am-

28

putated, but a few days later he had caught pneumonia and died. Lord, they had all felt terrible about it. He and Wes had sat there and blubbered like babies when they'd heard the news.

"Hurry up — hurry along!" Hundreds of feet slapped through the dust, speeding in the direction of the town of Gettysburg.

Custis wanted Bekah to know what the last words of the powerful, praying man had been. *Let us cross over the river and rest under the shade of the trees.* It was like poetry, he thought, such a simple and peaceful command. Not exactly the sort of sentiment one might expect from the military genius who had once said that the rebel yell was the sweetest music he had ever heard.

6

THE SIGN ON CEMETERY HILL READ *ALL PERSONS USING firearms on these grounds will be prosecuted with the utmost vigor of the law.*

Bekah had seen these words so many times that she no longer saw them. On this last bright morning in June, she walked slowly among the graves, humming "Lorena" under her breath and feeling very much alive. She loved this beautiful, peaceful, and solitary place where bees bumbled drowsily through the clover, and where, above the soft weathered tilt of the tombstones, birds spilled their fluid song among the branches of the evergreens.

> Remember me as you pass by
> As you are now, so once was I
> As I am now, so shalt thou be
> Prepare for death, and follow me.

Most of the verses she knew by heart, but that one always sent a pleasant shiver through her. Tillie Pierce wouldn't come here because she said it was gruesome to walk around on top of dead people, but Tillie was such a timid soul. She'd never stick around to watch a fire or a fistfight — she'd always run for home. Bekah had told her what would be written on her tombstone.

> This is the end of a boring book.
> Nothing happened to Tillie. She wouldn't look.

Bekah could never make her friend understand why she liked to be here, reading the inscriptions and imagining how these vanished people had looked and lived and loved and died. She was related to so many of them. The family plot was here, Summerhills stretching back for generations. Her mother's ancestors, the Mayhews, were buried in Baltimore, and a schoolmate of Leander's had said that that made Mrs. Summerhill a Copperhead, a traitor to the Union. Bekah knew it wasn't true. Maryland was a border state, and the people there had mixed feelings about the war, some leaning North, and others South. Yet in spite of strong family feelings and her loyalty to Aunt Mercy and the boys, her mother was on the side of the Union, Bekah knew.

> I've run my race, my pilgrimage
> How short my life, how swift my days
> My years are few, and ended soon
> My morning sun is set at noon.

It was hard to explain the pull of it. Maybe it was the mystery of death that brought her here, because someday. . . . But her mind always stopped short of believing in that someday. A brother and sister were buried here, but they had died as infants and Bekah could hardly remember their blurred baby faces. Father was here, too. His epitaph was simple, "Rest in Peace." Maybe that was why she liked to come so often, just to be close to him again. He had taught botany classes at Gettysburg College, and she had all of his old texts at home, with his fine scribbled notations in the margins, and his notebooks full of delicate sketches of flowers and plants. He had died of consumption not long after Buck joined the army. A quiet man, soft-spoken except when he spoke out hard-voiced against slavery.

"Freedom," he had told her once, "is a beautiful word, the most beautiful in any language. It's the only one worth dying for. Some people can't understand it or value it or honor or believe in it, but it's as essential to the spirit as air is to the body. If we take

31

away another person's freedom, then we deny our own humanity."

She had remembered his words recently when she had seen Aunt Beckie, who did washing for the Montforts, pushing a wheelbarrow down the pike with all her possessions piled crazily, a broken rocking chair upended on the top. As a little girl Bekah had heard her tell stories of growing up in Georgia, of having to pretend to be what the white folk who owned her expected her to be — grinning and backward and ignorant. Now the woman was frightened and crying. "No rebel is going to catch me and carry me back to be a slave again!"

Poor thing, Bekah thought, hadn't she heard about the Emancipation Proclamation? "Nobody can do that to you now. Mr. Lincoln has freed all the slaves in the rebel states."

"Huh!" Aunt Beckie looked at her with big scared eyes. "You think they care down south what *he* say? He ain't their president no more. They got their own, and Mr. Davis knows they need black backs to stay in business, honey! And I've heard all the pretty reasons for this fightin', but it's *our* sweat, *our* blood, *our* pain that's at the bottom of it. That's what this war is all about!" Terrified, she had disappeared into the hills and not come back, and Bekah had wondered if maybe she had been right, that it was slavery alone that was the long deep root of the conflict.

Across the shallow valley to the west the cupola of the Lutheran Theological Seminary blazed white against the cloudless blue sky. There was always a lot of activity over there during commencement week, but that was over now, and all the students had gone home. It was quiet. Too quiet. Queerly, unexpectedly she sensed that something was about to happen. Her heart beat faster, her nerves tingled as she stood and listened, but all she could hear was the humming monotony of the bees, and the fluting birdsong in the branches of the trees. Far away she thought there might be another sound, but it was drowned out by the hard, rapid knocking in her chest. Quickly she passed through the red brick arches of the cemetery gateway and hurried toward the town.

Shortly before noon General John Buford, with two brigades of Union cavalry, rode into Gettysburg from the south. Women rushed from their porches to offer cool water and iced lemonade, cake, and sandwiches. Old ladies peeked from behind their window curtains and waved handkerchiefs, and men took off their hats and cheered. Boys and girls ran along beside columns of ruddy military men in neat blue uniforms. These troopers carried sabres and carbines and rode on gleaming well-fed horses.

"Now that's a real army," Dr. Kendlehart said to Dr. Horner at the Diamond. "All spit and polish. Now we have nothing to worry about."

On the corner of Washington and High, Bekah and Tillie stood in their light summer dresses with ribbons shining in their hair, and sang the same chorus of "The Union Forever" over and over until both of them were hoarse. Cavalrymen smiled and waved as they passed by down the street, and when they were out of sight Bekah hated to let go of the excitement. "Come on, let's follow them and see if they make camp!"

Tillie said what she always said. "I can't. My mother wouldn't like it."

"Neither would mine. *If* she knew."

"I'm going home and make bouquets for the soldiers."

"Bouquets! You'd be better off making biscuits. At least they could eat those." Giving up on Tillie, Bekah said, "Then I'll go alone."

She caught up with Leander and Charles McCurdy on the Chambersburg Pike near Seminary Ridge. General Buford had set up his headquarters in the Theological building, and in the fields nearby hundreds of cavalrymen were making camp. Bekah and the boys sat on a fence rail, fascinated by the sight of the men putting up the canvas tents. Soon soldiers were boiling coffee, washing and mending clothes, playing cards, reading and writing letters, talking, joking, eating, resting. A young officer with thick, black hair and a soft, dark beard sat cross-legged on the ground, shirtsleeves rolled to his elbows, sewing a button on his jacket. Bekah admired how skillfully he managed the needle. Her mother made a living for them as a seamstress, and Bekah, who was supposed to help out when she could, found it hard work just to knot a thread.

The man looked up to where she sat, her hair a

haze of fire where the hot sun touched it. He smiled, recognizing her.

" 'The Union Forever!' "

She smiled back, swinging her feet. "I know it must have seemed that way. My friend and I didn't know the second chorus, so we just kept singing the first one!"

"Are you going to be here long?" Leander hopped down from the fence, followed by Charles.

"That depends."

"On what?"

The officer had finished with the button, and he put away the needle in the mending kit soldiers called their housewife. "On the rebels. That's why we're scouting now . . . to find out what they're up to."

"Where are they?" Bekah asked.

"Some are coming down from the north, and others are moving in this way from the west."

"Where is the rest of our army?"

"It's coming up fast from the south."

"But all the roads lead to Gettysburg," Bekah said. "And if everyone gets here at the same time, there'll be a fight, won't there?"

"Yes," he said carefully, "there could be."

"But where?" She looked around her at the quiet woodlands and sunny pastures. "There's no place here for a battle, is there?"

"Look over there." He came and stood beside the fence, pointing across the green and gold patches in the valley, the neatly tended trees in Sherfy's peach

35

orchard. "That's good ground south of town." His eyes moved from Cemetery Hill along the high ridge to where it ended about a mile away in two wooded knobs. "And when you fight, it's better to grab hold of good ground and defend it than to have to attack from a place that isn't quite as good. Here, for instance. See how much longer this ridge is than the one over there? It would be harder to move troops back and forth, and there isn't the high ground at the ends to anchor the line."

"If we did fight, and we did win, would the war be over then?"

"Yes, if we destroyed their army."

She did not want to think of that, of Custis and Mason being destroyed.

Leander asked, "But what if they won?"

"It could still be over. People are very tired of this war. If we lost here, on our own soil, it's possible the North might be discouraged enough to give in and give General Lee what he wants . . . recognition of the Confederacy."

"Then we have to win," Bekah said.

"We do." His gray eyes were steady, reassuring. "And we will. Try not to worry about it. Chances are nothing will happen here anyway. Even if something does, you folks will be safe in town."

"I'm not worried." Bekah took a scrap of paper and a stub of pencil from her pocket. "Our name is Summerhill." She scribbled an address. "And here's where we live, just in case you might need anything.

My mother won't mind. She'd want you to ask. You see, my brother Buck is in the army, too."

"My name is Adam Waite. I'm a schoolteacher from Batavia, New York. And you're very kind." He took the paper, and put it into his pocket. "But I hope by morning we'll be far away from here, and you'll never have to lay eyes on us again."

"Captain Waite!" A messenger hurried toward them. "You're to report to General Buford, sir. Rebels have just been sighted out along the pike."

The officer slipped into his jacket and buttoned it quickly. "You three had better skedaddle."

"What does that mean?" Bekah asked, as he left.

"Retreat, of course." Charles was related to John Reynolds, a well-known Pennsylvania general, and liked to think he knew all the military terms.

People slept better that night with the comforting blue presence of the cavalry blanketing the fields northwest of town. During the afternoon General Buford had sat calmly on his horse at the Diamond and carefully surveyed all the roads that led into Gettysburg, and later he had been seen on Cemetery Hill, staring out across the valley at the long, curving spine of Seminary Ridge. In spite of the rumors that rebels had been seen along the Chambersburg Pike, the general had appeared serene and unworried.

Actually, Buford was very concerned. There were holes in his information. Why was Lee suddenly drawing in his scattered forces? What about the riders who had appeared on the outskirts of town and then skittishly withdrawn when they spotted his troopers? All his military instincts warned him that there was real danger here.

"It's nothing to worry about," one of his men had said. "Our patrols will take care of them if they come back."

"No, you can't," Buford argued. "They will attack you in the morning, and they will come booming, three deep. You'll have to fight them like the devil until supports arrive!"

Until supports arrive. That was the problem that bothered him the most. Between eighty and ninety thousand Federal troops were on their way, with the First and the Eleventh Corps only a few hours distant, but if the trouble started before they arrived he would have to hold off the enemy with only two thin brigades. The cavalry was the eyes of the army, and its job was to scout, not to fight, but he had trained his men to dismount in a skirmish; one man was to hold the horses, leaving three others free to use the new fast-firing carbines. That special training might come in very handy on the following day.

At least he knew where the good ground was — and the importance of holding on to it until the Union forces reached Gettysburg.

July 1

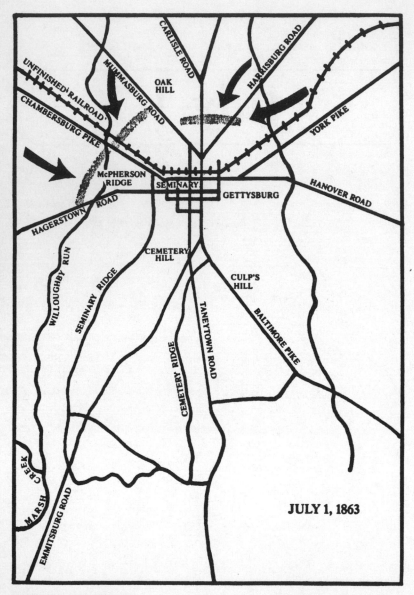

CARLISLE ROAD

HARRISBURG ROAD

UNFINISHED RAILROAD

MUMMASBURG ROAD

OAK HILL

CHAMBERSBURG PIKE

YORK PIKE

McPHERSON RIDGE

SEMINARY

HAGERSTOWN ROAD

GETTYSBURG

HANOVER ROAD

WILLOUGHBY RUN

SEMINARY RIDGE

CEMETERY HILL

CULP'S HILL

CEMETERY RIDGE

TANEYTOWN ROAD

BALTIMORE PIKE

MARSH CREEK

EMMITSBURG ROAD

JULY 1, 1863

UNION
CONFEDERATE

7

A MISTY RAIN MADE IT DIFFICULT TO SEE. NEAR WIL-
loughby Run, west of Seminary Ridge, Corporal Alphonse Hodge peered through the fine chilling
drizzle, waiting for the dawn. Night duty was longer,
colder, lonelier than any other time. More frighten-
ing, too. Many times since midnight he had heard
those silky rustlings, those mysterious snaps and
cracks of sound that aroused him from drowsiness,
quickened his heartbeat. The rebels were skilled in
surprise attacks, and could pounce with that savage
yell that was as much a weapon as were their muskets. Hodge was relieved to see the first light blooming faintly through the branches. He wanted coffee,
sweet and scalding in a metal cup. Soon he could
sleep.

His eye caught movement, lost it, then retrieved
it — fluid uncertain shapes flowing through the fog
along the pike. Instantly alert, he whispered to the
others; he sent one of the pickets hurrying to the left,
another to the right, and one to the rear to inform the
reserve line. Moving quickly, Hodge splashed across
the shallow creek to have another look. A minie ball

whined past his ear and splatted into the dripping foliage that straggled along the creek bed behind him.

Confederates. Coming in early, as John Buford had expected.

His orders were not to return fire, but as the corporal withdrew he stopped by the side of the road and tore off three quick rounds with his carbine before he sped away with his report.

Leander made it to the front door without making a noise, but as his hand clutched the knob he was seized by the back of the neck.

"Where are you going?"

"Shhhhhhhh." He was annoyed that Bekah had caught him. "Out to the camp. Let go!"

"I'm coming, too."

Leander squirmed free, started to argue, and then changed his mind. If their mother heard them, then neither of them would go. He wished his sister would act her age, take up embroidery or religion, anything that would keep her out of his hair. Bekah had an unnatural interest in knowing what was going on. "Curiosity killed the cat" their mother had told her many times, and Bekah always answered, "Yes, and satisfaction brought it back."

He hoped she was satisfied now that she'd spoiled his chance to slip out to the camp ground alone.

The morning air was fresh and cool. Rain during the night had rinsed the dusty town clean, and paint gleamed white and blue and yellow on the wooden houses along the street.

"What are you all dressed up for?" Leander asked. Bekah wore a starched pink and white gingham dress, and there were crisp pink ribbons looped through her dark red hair. Bekah didn't answer. She never answered when she didn't want to.

He said, "You want to see that captain again, don't you?"

They passed Mrs. McClellan's house with its white lattice fence. Inside an infant was roaring.

Bekah said cheerfully, "That baby sure can holler."

Men and boys were strolling out along the pike and collecting around the Seminary building. Some had fanned out across the road and were standing along the unfinished railroad cut that ran parallel to it. Leander and his friends called it the old Tapeworm Railroad.

"Listen. . . ." Bekah touched her brother's arm. They could hear faint sounds of gunfire in the direction of Marsh Creek, about three miles away. "What do you suppose that is?"

"The soldiers are practicing," Leander said. "They do it every morning." He didn't know if they did or not, but it seemed likely. Together he and Bekah walked out toward the camp they had visited the day before. Even at such an early hour it looked deserted, with only a few fires left smoldering. A guard, left on duty, was startled to see them and waved his arms. "Get out of here — quick! Go away! Go away!"

"We just want to know when the men will be back," Leander said.

"Don't ask questions! Skedaddle! Do you want to get your heads blown off?"

The gunfire sounded closer now and more intense, advancing in noisy bursts, a crackling dispute. Hurrying back toward the Seminary, Bekah saw men and boys climbing trees to get a better look.

"Come on, Leander — let's watch!" She swung herself up into the branches of an oak, disregarding her long, full skirts and the twigs that were pulling her ribbons loose. The gunfire was hotter now, getting even closer. Perched high, she could see a thin blue line along McPherson's Ridge moving slowly back in their direction. There was a strange, wild gliding whistle in the air, and a heavy explosion a few hundred yards away. Limbs, sheared from a tree, crashed to the ground.

"That's not practicing!" Bekah shouted to Leander. "It's a real fight, and we're in the middle of it!"

Spectators were dropping out of trees, jumping from fence rails, scattering along the Tapeworm Railroad cut, and dashing through the fields toward town. Bekah and Leander scrambled down through the branches and followed the crowd down the pike. They jumped to one side as an officer on horseback pounded past them. Bekah recognized him from a picture Charles McCurdy had shown her. "Leander, that's General Reynolds!"

Her brother didn't look back, but only sprinted faster down the turnpike.

* * *

"Thank God! Thank God!"

Buford, who had been watching anxiously from the cupola of the Seminary building, heard faint music piping south of town and saw, far in the distance, columns of soldiers moving rapidly in his direction, cutting across lots in their hurry.

He had not been wrong. The Confederates had come booming at dawn, and for two tense hours his cavalry brigades and a battery of artillery had managed to hold back the enemy. He was deeply relieved that help was finally on the way; his men were tired now, weakening fast. An aide rushed up to tell him that General Reynolds had arrived, and as Buford clattered down the stairs, he called out in greeting, "There's the Devil to pay!"

Chauncy Sullivan, an eighteen-year-old gunner, grinned as the men from the Iron Brigade plunged along the Chambersburg Pike with a long, swinging route step, their muskets shining in the sunlight. "You took your time getting here!"

"We wanted to give you fellows a chance to warm up the Johnnies for us!"

"Well, we did. They're hotter than firecrackers now."

Chauncy felt better as the tough, joking veterans with the familiar black slouch hats tilted down over their eyes poured past him up the road. In a blurred dawn a few shots had been exchanged, and suddenly a vicious little fight had developed. He and his crew had lobbed off shot and shell as fast as they could, and somehow the cavalry had managed to hold off an overwhelming enemy force. Now with the infantry on hand everyone could get down to the fine mean business of killing — and winning. Reynolds was a good man, smart and experienced, and with the First Corps coming the battle would soon be under control.

"Hurry. And tell *them* to hurry." General Reynolds sent a courier in search of the Eleventh Corps, and another message to Meade in Taneytown, fifteen miles away, promising to hold Gettysburg as long as possible. George Meade had just been appointed to replace Joe Hooker — an unexpected choice. Reynolds had been offered the chance to command the Army of the Potomac himself and had turned it down, so the President had ordered Meade to take it.

No, this was what he liked to do. Reynolds was where he wanted to be, exhilarated, sharpened, cool in the clatter of battle, thinking fast, moving quickly, crisply rapping out orders. He couldn't fail here. This was Pennsylvania, home soil.

Buford withdrew his battered line, and Reynolds ordered the Iron Brigade into McPherson's woods and another brigade to the north. He was leading more men into the trees south of the pike when he slid from his horse, and lay sprawled on the ground.

"He's dead! My God, the general's been killed."

"What did you say?" Chauncy Sullivan called after the soldier running down the road. *"Reynolds?"*

"Dead!" The soldier ran on.

Sullivan sagged against the big gun, wiping his face with the back of his arm. It was still early morning, and yet night had already fallen on a brilliant officer. Too soon, and bad, bad luck.

Bodies in blue and gray and butternut filled the swales, lifted over rises, spread out along McPherson's Ridge, through woods and open fields; panting men splashed across Willoughby Run, faces grimy with powder, greasy with sweat, firing, reloading, running ahead through screeching missiles and whistling minie balls.

"Here come those damned black-hatted fellers again!" screamed an Alabaman, as troops from Wisconsin and Michigan and Indiana plowed into the fight. Something startling occurred to him. Since dawn he had thought they were up against inexperienced Gettysburg boys. "It ain't no local militia!" He had seen these men before in battle. "It's the Army of the Potomac!"

Federal soldiers crossed the turnpike, advanced on the unfinished railroad cut, and were blasted down in rows. Those who made it that far riddled the Confederates trapped in the trench into a sodden pulpy mass. Regimental colors flashed and faded through a thickening haze; horses shrieked in agony and fell, spraying blood. The deep-chested Union cheer and the shrill rebel yell mingled across a widening, bleeding arc of combat.

Chauncy Sullivan stared in wonder as an old man in a swallowtail coat and a funny, high hump of a hat stumped down the pike past the battery and calmly shouldered his way in among the veterans in the woods. Nobody questioned John Burns, who was carrying the musket he had used in the war of 1812 and the Mexican war. Somebody handed him a better gun, and he went to work.

8

THERE WAS A QUICK TAP AT THE DOOR AND A bright-cheeked girl of twenty stepped inside the house. "Mrs. Summerhill? I hate to bother you at a time like this, but we're almost out of flour. Would you be able to spare a little?"

"Of course, Jennie. We have plenty. How's the dear baby?"

"Doing just lovely, thanks. . . . And making more racket inside than anything happening out there." Jennie Wade had a wide, serene smile. "My mother and sister are worried. I keep telling them that nothing will happen to us, that it's the poor souls fighting out on the ridge that. . . ." Her voice drifted off toward the back of the house as the two women went into the kitchen.

Bekah stood looking out the parlor window, listening to the heavy explosions in the west, and the steady driving rattle of gunfire that sounded like hail on a roof. Outside there was confusion, helter-skelter movement; dogs ran barking in all directions, and children who had escaped from their houses were being chased back indoors. Earlier Bekah had seen Charles McCurdy and his family taking refuge with his grandmother, who lived a few doors away, and he had told her that the houses on Chambersburg Street, in the direct line of battle, were being vacated. Union troops were still rushing past, and neighbors were offering water to the hot and thirsty soldiers as they passed by on the double-quick. Bekah and Leander had been kept busy rushing from the pump to the curb and back again, carrying buckets and dippers, but as the first wounded began coming in from the fields, some walking, some helped by comrades, some carried in on litters, Bekah had retreated to the house. There were two things in the world that frightened her, and one was the sickly slippery sight of blood.

Jennie Wade came back down the hallway, carrying half a sack of flour. Bekah called out softly, "Have you heard from Jack yet?"

Jennie ducked her head into the parlor. "Not yet, Bekah."

"You'll hear soon." Mrs. Summerhill patted the young woman's shoulder. "I'll be making up that wedding dress any day. Now kiss that baby for me, will you?"

"I will. And thank you!"

Outside the house an officer on horseback called to

Jennie, "Better stay indoors, miss. Go down to your cellar. It's the safest place."

She smiled up at him, the sunlight glistening on her high crown of braided hair. "I'm not afraid."

"Please, don't take chances." He watched her as she walked without hurry toward her sister's small, brick house behind the lattice fence. "You too, Ma'am," he said to Mrs. Summerhill. "Stay inside with your children. Go to the cellar."

"Look!" Leander shouted from the curb. "Rebels!"

Prisoners were being hustled by under guard, sullen, dirty, and dejected men. Several were bloodstained and limping, and one had his pant leg torn away.

"Leander, come into the house!" his mother called.

A woman with a crying child in her arms hurried past, followed by a pale girl tugging a sobbing youngster by the hand.

"Tillie!" Bekah called from the open parlor window. "Where are you going?"

Tillie Pierce wailed, "Oh, Bekah . . . I'm so frightened! Mrs. Shriver wants me to go out to the Weikert farm with her, and my folks said I should go, but I'm scared!"

"Go ahead, Tillie — that's out by the Round Tops, you'll be safe there. Hurry!" As her friend disappeared along the congested street, Bekah felt a pang for Tillie who would, as usual, miss out on everything. *Nothing happened. She wouldn't look.*

"Bekah, we're going down to the cellar."

"Mother!"

"You heard me."

"But we won't be able to see anything down there."

"This minute!"

Bekah sighed, and closed the window. In the kitchen her mother was putting plates and cutlery into a basket, along with some cold baked beans and cheese. In the confusion of the morning she had burned a pan of biscuits, but she put these in too. "Leander, you'd better carry down a jug of milk."

There was a banging at the front door. Bekah looked down the hall. A bearded face stared back at her through the glass. Leander pushed past his sister. "It's that army captain!"

The man leaned against the jamb, a scrap of paper in his fingers. "Summerhill?"

Leander helped him inside. Bekah felt queasy at the sight of the smashed and bleeding arm, the dark blood soaking through his torn jacket.

"Leander — go and find Dr. Horner!" Mrs. Summerhill whipped off her apron, and pressed it gently against the streaming wound. "Hurry now, before this poor man bleeds to death. Tell him he must come. Quick, Bekah — get me towels, or whatever you can find!"

Adam Waite lay in the high feather bedstead in Buck's room under clean sheets that were already soaked with red. The doctor's hands were quick, his orders brief. "Come here, Bekah — I'll need your help."

"Shouldn't Mother. . . ?"

"Her nerves won't stand the strain. I've told her to rest and stay quiet, and you must make sure she does just that. So far as our patient here goes, my girl, you're it."

"Yes, sir."

She had never fainted in her life and never intended to, but as Bekah approached the bed she felt her knees dissolving. Quickly she grabbed hold of the bedpost.

"The bone in the upper arm is broken, but that's no real problem . . . it's the lower arm. . . . I could go in after that ball, but the procedure takes time . . . a great deal of time. . . ."

Bekah knew he was thinking of all the wounded men coming into town, needing care.

The captain opened his eyes. "Please, Doctor." His voice was tired and weak, difficult to understand. "I need the arm."

"I know . . . I know. . . ." The physician probed gently, mumbling to himself as he made his examination. "But the ball is in so deep. It will be dangerous and painful, very, very painful to go after it. And I can't be sure that your arm will mend safely, it's so badly torn. . . . The simplest thing to do would be to remove the arm below the elbow."

The captain was suffering. Bekah could feel his pain in the clenched pit of her stomach. She tried not to look at the blood puddling the sheets or at the mangled flesh.

Dr. Horner glanced up at her. He had made up his mind. "I'm going to try and get that ball, Bekah, and I'll want you to give him some chloroform. At least we can put him out of his misery for a while." He handed her a small brown bottle and a wad of cotton from his surgical case, and told her what to do. Bekah would have liked to take a whiff and put herself out of *her* misery, but the wounded man was staring at her with hopeful gray eyes and she knew she must do as she was told. As she uncorked the bottle a strong odor escaped, making her head spin.

"Breathe deeply, Captain," Dr. Horner said. As soon as she sensed that her patient had lost consciousness, Bekah took away the saturated cotton, and tightly recorked the bottle.

"Good . . . very good." The doctor was concentrating. "Women have been helping out, you know . . . in the Washington hospitals. I believe they make excellent nurses, as good as the men, though some people feel there are certain things no refined female should ever do or see. Now, if you'll open the curtains as wide as you can — I'll need all the light I can get."

Unexpectedly the fear was gone. Bekah came back from the window and watched as Dr. Horner worked. He was breathing hard, his fingers as sure and swift and delicate as her mother's were when she did fine embroidery, yet she did not see how he could ever make that broken, bleeding mass whole again. It was taking a very long time. She took a towel, and touched it lightly to his forehead. "I can fix your spectacles for you if you can spare them for a minute. . . . They're getting misted."

"Please."

Bekah wiped and then replaced them. The doctor bent his head again, his breath coming in little puffs. There was a metallic sound as a smashed gray object dropped into the enamel pan. "Got it!"

He beamed up at her. "It's lucky that Leander found me when he did. I was on my way to the Lutheran Church. They're using it as a hospital. Out on the field, you see, they would have cut off the arm. . . . There would never be time for this sort of thing." He worked patiently, talking softly as he stitched. "Bandages, Bekah. Tear up clean towels or sheets, that's the good girl. Then our patient must rest. I'll give you some drops for his pain. Stay with him as much as you can. He'll want fluids when he's conscious. I'm not sure when I can get back to see him. I suspect there's a long, bloody day ahead for all of us."

It was finished. Dr. Horner stood up, eased his back, and then washed his hands at the commode. He smiled at Bekah as she handed him a fresh towel. "I hope we did the right thing, Bekah. I hope by saving the arm we haven't lost the man. One never knows. I'm going to leave him in your hands, and good, strong, capable hands they are. To think it was only yesterday that I brought you into the world, and look at you now, a grown-up young lady."

She said shyly, "I'll be sixteen on Saturday."

"The Fourth of July." He called to her as he went down the stairs, "Let's hope there's a country left to celebrate on the Fourth of July."

9

AT CHAMBERSBURG GENERAL LEE TRIED TO MAKE sense out of the reports coming in to him. On Tuesday Pettigrew's men had headed into Gettysburg to find some desperately needed shoes; they had seen a few enemy uniforms and had reported back to General Heth. Convinced that what they had seen was probably the local militia, Heth had agreed to let Pettigrew return for the shoes the next morning. That was how it had started. Now a little skirmish had developed into something bigger.

As he pressed Traveller to reach Gettysburg quickly, Lee hoped that the Old Soldier's Disease, which was draining his energy, wouldn't be a nuisance to him much longer. He was feeling his age these days. It was as if his body, once fit and healthy and uncomplaining, nagged him for attention. First the heart and the troubling shortness of breath, and then this annoying dysentery. It worried him not to be in peak condition. A victory here and it was possible the war might end.

A. P. Hill, the commander of the Third Corps, was waiting, his bearded face blotched with red, twitching nervously above the collar of the crimson shirt he liked to wear into battle. He admitted that the brigades had met some surprising resistance on their shopping trip to town that morning. "But I have another division ready to go in and back up Heth. Dorsey Pender's men . . . good fellows." Hill was usually unsettled during military operations, but on this bright July morning Lee thought the man really looked quite ill as he repeated that he had men ready to go in. "With your permission, sir."

"Wait. Wait. . . ." Lee would not be rushed into this. He moved to and fro on his horse, listening to the familiar crack of muskets and the steady rumble of artillery, straining to understand what lay behind it. Heavy casualty reports were coming in now, and word had arrived that General Archer had been taken prisoner. In spite of his composure a hot cone of anger against his cavalry burned in his chest. No, he was not angry with them, but with his favorite, Jeb Stuart, the officer who had let him down. He had known that the marvelous man had flaws, that he was sometimes too buoyant and reckless, but this time he was unforgivably late, and Lee felt like a blinded man. He did not know what the danger was or where it was located. For all he knew, the soldiers scrambling through the woods and fields northwest of town might be involved with the whole Army of the Potomac. A spy had reported columns of the enemy in the area, but he knew he wasn't ready yet for a major encounter, not until all of his troops had arrived.

Hill said, "Just give me the word, sir. Pender will clear the road for us in no time."

"Not yet." The general never minded taking risks when he had to, but he refused to be stupid. "Let's wait and see just what it is we're up against."

And so a lull occurred, a little yawn in time, even as the snap of musketry went on and shells continued to burst and blossom white against the innocent blue sky. Time for parched soldiers to swallow tepid water and exhausted gun crews to reposition batteries and replenish ammunition, as a long slow scarf of yellow smoke drifted across the damaged ground.

Then, abruptly, things began to happen again. The murky puzzle that was baffling Lee came together sharply with a sudden shape and clear design. Five brigades of Rodes's division appeared north of the pike on Oak Hill in exactly the right position to swoop down on the tired blue troops that faced the west. If Pender drove in now with his fresh supports, and Rodes's men slammed down hard from the hill, the Union line would have to give. Integral parts clicked smoothly into place as if they had been planned. General Lee, his instincts for opportunity humming, gave the orders.

Yet Federal gears were whirring, too. The Eleventh Corps had just arrived, men fresh for battle hurrying double-quick along the pike and fanning out north of town. It was a hard luck unit, the scapegoat of the army because of its large number of immigrant recruits, but this time it was fortunate. The Confederates rushing down from Oak Hill came too fast, too eagerly, and the Eleventh hurled them back and forced them to regroup. Now the war machine boomed heavily across the landscape, knocking down fence rails, blasting wildflowers, smashing thousands of men under as it rumbled through the sultry summer afternoon.

"Rebekah!" Her mother called from below. "Come down to the cellar! Something terrible is going on outside!"

"I'm coming!" Bekah called, but she had no intention of leaving the captain. Besides, she had to see what was happening. From the window she watched Union soldiers running, chased by the rebels. Blue bodies dangled from fence tops, were thrown down in gutters, sprawled motionless in alleys and yards, on doorsteps and porches. Shocked and disbelieving, she watched the deadly game, thinking of Buck, wondering if he were being stalked through the streets he had played in when he was a boy.

The wounded man moaned and tossed his head restlessly upon the pillow. His black hair was damp and tangled. The heavily bandaged arm, held in a sling, was stained dark with his blood. Bekah went to him and wiped his face with a cool damp cloth. The smell of chloroform clung to him. He groaned and moved beneath the sheet, murmuring something that she couldn't understand. She heard one word distinctly spoken. *Anna.*

The Eleventh had fought well as they struggled to keep in touch with the seasoned First Corps still stubbornly facing west. Then, once again, the unexpected happened. More rebel troops arrived right in the place where they could do the most damage. Jubal Early, the general that Lee affectionately called his bad old man, had sent in men on three sides of the exposed right flank of the Union line, and in an odd quirk of battle what should have been a retreat became instead a panicky rout. It had happened before — in May, at Chancellorsville, when Stonewall Jackson had surprised the Eleventh and sent them flying in terror. Now, at the raw, bleeding stump-end of the afternoon, the corps did what others said they always did. Ran. Stampeded. Breathless, gasping, a jumble of frantic soldiers pounded back into the streets of Gettysburg, tumbling into alleys and back lanes, diving into barns and outhouses, hiding under woodpiles and in pigsties, banging desperately on closed doors, followed by the crackle of rifleshot and shrieking shells and the eerie, scalping yell of the pursuing rebels.

"Run, you bluebellies — you cowards — run!"

Adam Waite cried out in pain, and Bekah left the window and returned to his bedside. He was still unconscious, perspiration beaded on his face, and she wrung out another cloth and folded it across his forehead. There was a sharp crack, and glass exploded violently into the room, jagged pieces shattering against the walls and floor, scattering across the bottom of the bed.

"Are you all right?" Leander stood in the doorway, staring at Bekah with eyes like burned holes in a blanket.

She was amazed that she was, and that the captain hadn't been touched.

"Look." Leander pointed at a chunk of minie ball smeared gray against the wall above the bed.

There was a noisy banging down below. Through the smashed window Bekah saw men in gray and butternut moving quickly from house to house, demanding to be let in to search for Union soldiers. Rebels were dragging prisoners out into the streets, rounding them up in groups, and taking them away.

"Bekah, someone is at the door," Mrs. Summerhill said, coming into the bedroom, "and I can't let them in. They'll murder us all . . . or worse."

She was shaking from head to foot, holding her arms rigidly against her body to stop the trembling.

"Stay here with Leander," Bekah said. "I'll go and see who it is."

As soon as she opened the door she recognized the soldier. It was the courteous boy she had given Buck's boots to, but he looked older and taller, stretched by the authority of his loaded gun. "I have orders to search the house, miss."

"No."

"Please, miss." He spoke softly, glancing nervously over his shoulder into the street. "The lieutenant says we have to bring out any soldiers who are hiding indoors."

"We're not hiding any. There's a man upstairs who is hurt, but he's feeling so poorly that he'll die if he's moved, and I'm not going to let that happen. He's my special charge," she explained. "The doctor asked me to care for him, and I promised that I would."

"Better let me in, then." He was trying to tell her something with his eyes. She stepped aside, and closed the door after him.

"You give me your word there's only a sick man upstairs?"

"It's the truth."

"Then you won't be bothered no more. That's a promise."

She let out a long, shaky breath. "You still look hungry. Are you?"

"Haven't had much since you fed me so fine a few days ago."

"Wait here." She ran down to the cellar, and scooped up the batch of biscuits and a jar of apple butter. When she returned he was standing motionless in the hall, his floppy hat held in his hands. "I'm sorry these are burned. We weren't expecting company."

He shoved a biscuit into his mouth, and crammed the rest into his pocket. He put the apple butter inside his uniform jacket and buttoned it out of sight.

"You've been right kind, miss. Them boots have been a comfort to me." He went to the door. "And I'm sorry if I scared you."

Her chin went up. "Why, you didn't scare me at all."

Unsupported, the First Corps was forced to retreat as well, but these soldiers backtracked coolly, firing over their shoulders as they went, avoiding the massacre in the streets as they made their way to the safety of Cemetery Hill, a few hundred feet south of town.

By four-thirty in the afternoon Confederate colors blazed at the Diamond. The town was now in the possession of the Army of Northern Virginia. Through his field glasses General Lee had watched the Federal withdrawal; he knew that victory was in his hands if the pursuit was quickly followed up before the Union troops became entrenched on the high ground. He sent off a message to Ewell, the man who had replaced Stonewall Jackson. It was only necessary to push those people, he wrote, to get possession of the heights. He would like the general to take the hill if practicable.

Dick Ewell knew who Lee meant by *those people*. It was the gentle phrase he always used to describe the enemy. It was the *if practicable* that confused him. He dithered. He was hot and tired and the stump of the leg he had lost at Manassas rubbed painfully against the clumsy wooden peg he wore. His men were worn out, and rumors were coming in that Union troops were coming down from the north. If the commander wanted the hill taken, why didn't he say so outright? This message didn't sound like a direct order. Since it was now up to him, then he would leave things as they were.

Along the high protective ridge, more of *those people* were pouring in, hastily scooping out rifle pits. On Cemetery Hill, young Chauncy Sullivan helped the crew to position the big guns, and then he flopped wearily to the ground, too tired to boil coffee, too exhausted to eat. Finally he reached into his knapsack, and fumbled for a handful of crackers. One of the artillerymen packed a pipe and then sat down beside him, glancing shrewdly at his bleak face. "Things ain't so bad."

"No."

"Support's coming up real fast now."

"Yes."

"We hurt 'em today."

Chauncy grunted. "They hurt *us.*"

"It was an orderly retreat . . . I mean the First Corps, not them other scared rabbits."

Chauncy chewed, looking thoughtful. Someone handed him a cup of coffee, and he drank it slowly, gratefully.

The other man sighed, stretched out on the ground, puffing peacefully on his pipe. Chauncy felt a deep uneasiness, a troubling sadness. It was the thought of the cheerful men he had seen swinging loosely into battle that morning. Now most of them were dead or wounded. The Iron Brigade, one of the most dependable fighting units in the army, had been almost wiped away.

From where he sat, on high ground or not, things did not look so good.

10

"THEY SAY THERE'S BEEN FIGHTING AT GETTYSBURG ... that General Reynolds has been killed." Buck's mouth was sanded dry. He tasted grit in his mouth, felt it in his eyes and hair, sifting in through the pores of his skin. Inside him marched a dry, white man of dust. "I've been worrying about my folks, Tully. I hope they're all right."

Tully had nothing to say. The 83rd slogged on in the direction of Hanover, men swinging one foot ahead of the next as the band coaxed them along with "Yankee Doodle."

Buck didn't expect any answer. He kept on talking because he thought it was the right thing to do, like not letting a man with a concussion go to sleep. He had to keep Tully going until he could find someone who might help him. His folks lived in Erie now. Maybe there was some way to reach them.

His eyes moved back and forth across the blooming summer landscape. He felt excitement building, like a pressure in his chest. "Looks like we're really going home, Tull. It's beautiful, isn't it? Just the way I remember it."

Tully thought Buck was just plain crazy. *Beautiful?* Cautiously, as if the sight might hurt his eyes, he peered around him, ready to duck down again inside his shirt. *Beautiful!* This country was hostile, hot, hard. Corn stood in tense green ranks, leaves bristling sharp as bayonets. Cabbages in the fields were weapons ready to explode; in menacing orchards he saw small green apples meanly concealed in the branches. Platoons of tiger lilies paraded in the ditches, their brassy throats like the trumpets that ripped him out of sleep at reveille. Overhead was the cruel commanding eye, the sun.

Buck went on talking. "They say that Little Mac is back in charge, but I don't believe it. McClellan's finished with this army, Tull. I've thought about it, and wondered why we failed him, but now I think maybe it was the other way around. Course nobody took better care of us than he did. You recall how much we admired and respected him, don't you? Remember the time he inspected us, and he said to Colonel McLane, 'I congratulate you on having one of the best regiments in the army.' Remember how we cheered! Every man of us would have died for him then."

Tully did not want to hear what his friend was saying. Silently he ducked his head lower, his eyes fixed on the road ahead, away from the threatening meadows. Buck was always trying to look for reasons, find meaning in things even as nonsensical as the war.

"The way I see it, Tull . . . he just wouldn't take chances. He was afraid to use us. We could have done anything if he'd felt sure of himself. We trusted him — why couldn't he trust us? There wasn't so much wrong with us. . . . There was something missing in him, and you know what that was, Tull?" Buck paused a moment, and then answered himself. "Imagination. He wanted the battles planned out in advance like a diagram in a textbook, and we know it doesn't happen that way. Battles make themselves up as they go along, and that's something Lee understands. You've got to move with them, guess what's going to happen somewhere before it does."

There had been too many hesitations and defeats. These men he marched with were capable soldiers, and one day they would know it.

They were approaching Hanover and people were coming out of their houses, running to the sides of the road to offer food and drink. Buck felt a deep, joyful sense of homecoming. A pretty girl ran up to him and threw a chain of daisies around his neck, and he blushed with pleasure, feeling the hot color rise into his cheeks. He turned and watched until her pleasing, rounded shape was out of sight. He thought of Jennie Wade, with her wholesome vanilla fragrance. With every step he was drawing closer to her. But she would marry Jack Skelly and be lost to him forever, without ever knowing how much he loved her.

On the outskirts of town they stopped briefly to rest. Rumors spread among the men about the battle at Gettysburg, and Buck felt a mixture of anticipation and anxiety. Leander was young, too young to look out for his mother and sister. Buck was impatient to move, to get back on the road, to reach home.

Johnson's men had been held up at Greenwood when fifteen miles of Confederate soldiers and horses and wagons had collided with the main body of troops coming in from Chambersburg. By the time the knot of confusion had been untied the Stonewall Brigade had been delayed for hours. When it reached Gettysburg, late in the afternoon, it was too late to get in on the fight.

North of town the men faced a thickly wooded hill. It looked unoccupied and they expected they would be ordered to take it, but when no command came to advance they ate their suppers and then stretched out to rest. Wes Culp found a spring bubbling close to the camp where he scrubbed his face and hands. Then, taking a toothbrush from his pocket, he carefully cleaned his teeth.

"I can hardly believe it." Custis was sprawled on the ground, with his slouch hat tilted down to the sleepy blue slits of his eyes. "Wes Culp . . . primping!"

"I'm going to town, Cus. General Walker has given me special permission to go and see my sisters."

"Now how did a little fellow like you ever manage to reach as high as him?"

"His orderly is a friend of mine, and he fixed it up."

Custis untangled his bare feet, sat up, and then rose slowly to his full height. He looked down at Wes, and patted his head approvingly. "The thing I like about you, son, is the way you do things *right,* permission and all. I never did get the hang of doing things that way. You set me a good example."

Wes grinned. "I try. I surely try." He smoothed his hair and beard, tugged down his soiled jacket, looked sadly at the rip in the sleeve of his uniform. "Now don't go waiting up for me, Mother dear."

"I wasn't planning on it. I'm going with you."

"Cus, you don't have a pass!"

"But I'm real good at doing things the *wrong* way."

"What if you get caught?"

Custis threw up his hands in horror. "Heavens! You mean I might get arrested or court-martialed — and not get a chance to fight tomorrow? Oh, that would hurt my feelings!"

"Be careful, please."

Happily Custis crossed his heart. "It just wouldn't be polite to be in the neighborhood and not drop in on my own kin. But I won't be late. Something tells me that that hill will be crawling with bluebellies tomorrow, and that's when they'll ask us to take it."

Wes smiled. "Take it? My family owns it. My Uncle Henry lives there now. That's Culp's Hill, Cus. That's where I was born."

* * *

"Tomorrow we can swing over there to the right." General James Longstreet gestured across the shadowed valley toward two rocky hills. "Move in around their left flank, get in on their rear, and then. . . ." He gripped his hands together, "We've got them!"

Everything about the big bearded man was solid and emphatic and logical, but this time he was wrong, and patiently Lee tried to explain one more time why the plan couldn't be tried. They still didn't know how many of *those people* were over there. If, as Longstreet suggested, they did maneuver around the Union troops, it was possible they might run into a loose piece of the army and leave themselves open to a shattering assault. Yet they just couldn't sit here and wait for something to happen. It was attack or withdraw, and they hadn't come all this way to pull back now.

The officer listened, shaking his head gloomily, his sad eyes held by the sparkle of the campfires beaded along the other ridge. "But we can find better ground than this," he argued. "Wait for them to attack *us*."

Lee wasn't surprised that Longstreet saw it this way. Many of the high-ranking commanders were subtle Virginians, but this one was a plain-spoken Georgian who enjoyed chewing over his theories on trench warfare with anyone who would listen. Old Pete they called him, and his instincts were defensive. Lee had been accused of that himself once, when he had ordered his men to dig in around Richmond early in his command. The King of Spades he'd been called, and he hadn't liked it much. Speed and surprise were the style of this whiplike army, and Stonewall's lightning strokes had helped lash that legend into life. Speed and crackling decisive moves and. . . .

Lee was very tired. The confusion of the day had drained him, and the dysentery weakened him. He felt as if his chest were packed with wool. The air was heavy, sultry, hard to breathe. He was pleased to have his most able corps commander here with him at last, reassured to know that all the troops would be in place on the following day, but he wasn't going to argue over what had already been decided. Even though Longstreet might disagree, he would always obey.

To change the subject he asked quietly, "How is Mrs. Longstreet, General?"

"Not so well." Old Pete's eyes, cool and unblinking, avoided Lee's sympathetic glance. Everyone had known personal tragedies during the war, but Lee thought that this handsome, trusted officer had suffered more than anyone he knew. Three of his children had been lost during one awful week of fever. The man was slower now, and heavier, his thoughts dragged down by grief.

"I am sorry." Lee would pray for him and his ailing wife again that night.

As they walked back toward headquarters in the small house near the Seminary building, Longstreet stopped and stared angrily across the valley, smacking his fist hard into his hand. "Why didn't Ewell go in and knock them off that hill when he had the chance! They're in solid by now. . . . They'll spend the whole night digging in, and they'll be waiting for us tomorrow to come to them!" His eyes flashed back to life. "But if we could lure them off that ridge and make them come to us. . . ."

The conversation took more energy than Lee could spare. Abruptly he ended it. "The enemy is there and I am going to attack him there."

"Here — over here!"

A lantern was lowered, a body prodded.

"Leave him be. It's in the belly. Let's pick up one who has a chance."

The light bobbed away. Glowing arcs crisscrossed the fields northwest of town. A great golden moon lifted, illuminating acres of destruction. Thousands of men had been killed or wounded or taken prisoner, and there were only a few hours of darkness for the burial and ambulance details to deal with the casualties before the battle heated up again.

"This one?"

"Naw. Chest's all tore up. Here, this one's leg is gone. Maybe they can save what's left of him."

Behind Union lines there was continuous restless motion. Wagons and ambulances rattled along the road, horses snorted softly, harnesses jingling. Officers rode back and forth, stopping to talk in low voices as they waited for General Meade to arrive from Taneytown. There were biting strokes of sound

71

from Culp's Hill, axes slashing through trees as soldiers hastily constructed breastworks all around the wooded slopes.

Across the valley fires blazed as the Southern soldiers boiled their coffee and cornmeal and joked among themselves. Their voices were dulled, drowsy. Wasn't it a caution the way those bluebellies had run again! The smell of victory hung in the smoky air, almost won today, sure to be theirs tomorrow. One by one the men rolled themselves into their blankets and sank to the bottom of sleep beneath the floating stars.

Three miles from Gettysburg, Buck Summerhill grinned when word was passed along the marching columns that someone had seen the spirit of George Washington riding by on his horse.

"It's an omen," said Jesse Flynn, awed by the news. "It means we're going to win tomorrow."

Buck did not believe in omens, good or bad. He took hold of Tully's arm. "Now watch out for that ghost manure, Tull. We don't want to slip in something we can't even see."

In the woods outside of town the men dropped heavily to the ground, and slept.

"Well, how do you feel?" Mrs. Burns asked her husband John. He sat propped in a chair, the coat of his old uniform folded across his knees, and from time to time he patted it as fondly as if it were an old dog.

"I feel like more whiskey, if you really want to know."

"That's for emergencies."

"Well, if fighting the rebels an' getting hit ain't an emergency, then I'd like to know what is!"

"You've had enough. It's time you went to bed."

"And how am I supposed to sleep with wild men yipping all over town? I'm going to rest a bit, and then I'm going to go and have another crack at 'em!"

"You're going to bed, John."

This time he kept his mouth shut. He knew that she had worried all the time he was gone. Then he'd come back, nicked in three places, with his tale of fighting with the army and being wounded and wandering into a rebel hospital by mistake, fooling them into treating him and letting him go.

She caught him grinning. "Now what's that about?"

"I was thinking of old Abe Lincoln. I'd like to tell him how it was today when I showed our black-hatted fellers a thing or two. It's the sort of story he'd enjoy."

"I dare say," she said sarcastically. "And the next time the President is in the neighborhood, why don't you ask him in and tell him all about it?"

No one would have guessed that he was always afraid, this lighthearted boy. In Pickett's camp at Chambersburg the mood was bright and relaxed as the soldier with straight clean features picked up a banjo and began to pluck rowdy music from the strings.

" 'Goober Peas,' Mason!"

" 'Dixie'!"

Soon there was a circle of men around him, clapping hands and slapping knees, hard brown faces softened by the leaping firelight.

"When Johnnie comes marching home again, hurrah, hurrah!
 We'll give him a hearty welcome then, hurrah, hurrah!
 The men will cheer, the boys will shout
 The ladies they will all turn out. . . ."

Mason Walker was seventeen years old. Since he had left home a year ago his delicate good looks had gradually faded, like the homespun pants and coat and battered hat he wore, until he no longer looked so very young. It was as if the youthful freshness had been rubbed away, revealing a plain, drab fabric underneath.

When he had been small his older brother Custis could make him weep just by teasing him, but now Mason took pride in knowing there was nothing that could make him cry.

He had been injured twice and had grown tough protective scars over painful though not serious wounds.

He was always afraid.

He still loved music, but the fine-boned hands that had caressed the piano in the parlor at home could load a gun in seconds, aim without flinching.

He was terrified of dying. Men more powerful than himself had set his course, military routines sharpened his edge, but he had a burning will to keep himself alive. He had stripped himself of nonessentials, reduced himself to blanket, musket, rations. His bright brown eyes were always observant and alert, missing nothing. He had learned a few tricks.

It was important not to care too much. Love and hate could tilt a man off balance, distract his judgment, open him to risk. Scraped of feelings, not thinking anymore of God or Cause or Honor, Mason prodded himself with sharp sticks of accusation, calling himself weak and cowardly, flogging himself to keep up with the rest in the same way he had once made himself keep up with Custis.

Foot stamping, fingers flying, he sang.

"And we'll all feel gay when Johnnie comes marching home!
And we'll all feel gay when Johnnie comes marching home!"

When the battle was over, the song would come true and they would march home with the war in their pockets. Pickett's Virginians. Men who belonged to a romantic tradition of courage and chivalry, who felt a special sense of place in the army. If he was careful nobody would ever know that he was a quaking coward in his heart.

11

A FULL MOON ROSE OVER ROOFTOPS, DRIFTED ABOVE the fields and meadowlands outside of town. Bekah, watching from Buck's room, could guess where its soft light fell, and thought such splendor seemed out of place that night.

Leander and her mother had gone to their beds, worn out from the excitement. Word had spread that Reverend Howell, a Union chaplain, had been shot to death on the steps of Christ Church, and the people were exhausted from shock and anger and fear. It had been the longest day of Bekah's life, and yet she was too tense, too coiled inside to sleep.

She went to the captain, and put her hand on his forehead, worried that the fever was a dangerous sign. What if something had gone wrong and he died in her care? But she wouldn't let him die. She stood looking down at him, willing him to stay alive.

"Anna. . . ." That name again, over and over. She wondered about the ghost woman who haunted his dreams. A flesh and blood Anna was miles away in New York State, unaware that he was calling for her.

Restless, she went back to the window. The air was thick and warm. Enemy soldiers lay spread-eagled on sidewalks, in yards and on porches. Some of them slept beside dead bodies in blue uniforms. From time to time patrols moved past, the soft Southern voices oddly foreign in the Yankee streets. Occasionally there was laughter, a drunken argument, a command. Rebels were billeted at the Court House; she could hear their voices and see campfires burning on the lawn. Everyone in town was proud of the new building, and Bekah hoped nothing would damage it.

She thought of Tillie Pierce, safe and asleep at the Weikert farm out by the Round Tops.

Downstairs there was a noise.

She listened, heard nothing more, let out her breath. Earlier she had heard the sound of splintering wood and breaking glass a few doors away and had guessed that someone was forcing an entrance into one of the abandoned houses.

Another muffled thump, deep in the basement, stealthy, human. Her heart rocked, her hand went to her throat. What if an enemy soldier had found his way in through an unlocked window? Even before the rebels had arrived she had been aware of a feminine fear among the older women as they talked in low voices across their backyard fences; she had wondered then what it was they were so afraid of. She sensed that it was some whispered violence, some deeper invasion of themselves too terrible for a young girl to understand, but nobody had told her what it was.

Footsteps squeaked on the basement steps. She tightened the belt of the flowered wrapper she had pulled on over her nightgown. Buck's squirrel gun was in his closet, and although it wasn't loaded she reached for it, and crept barefooted to the top of the stairs. Below she heard the cellar door pushed slowly open. Quietly it creaked shut. Some breathing thing, some *person* loomed tall within the thick gloom of the hall.

"Leave this house," she said in a low, hoarse whisper. "I have a gun. I'll blow your head off if you don't get out of here!"

There was a pause, then soft, delighted laughter.

"Bekah, you devil! After all the trouble I took to get here?"

"Who is it?"

"Come on down here and find out."

She couldn't see the face, but she knew that laughing voice and teasing tone. "Custis?" She flew down the stairs and into his arms. "Custis — it is you! Oh, I was scared!"

"Scared?" Gently he took the gun away from her and set it against the wall. "Bekah, I can't recall one single thing that ever frightened you."

She didn't mention the blood. She was used to it now, so it didn't count. "Spiders," she admitted. "Fat speckled ones with hair."

"If only I'd known a few years ago. I'd have made your life miserable." He lifted her off the floor and swung her in a circle.

"Put me down, Custis. I want to wake Mother and tell her that you're here."

"Honey, there isn't time for that. It's you I've come to see. Come in here. . . ." He led her into the front parlor, and closed the door behind them. "Let's have a look at you."

"They've shut off the gas. I'll light a lamp."

"No, someone might see. Over here by the window."

Moonlight streamed over them like dazzling dust, lighting their eager faces. Bekah thought he looked half wild with his gaunt face and shaggy spill of hair, but his eyes were the bright remembered blue, his tilted smile the same.

"Bekah. . . ." He was happily amazed. "You're all grown up and beautiful!"

"I'll be sixteen on Saturday."

"You didn't think I'd forget your birthday, did you?"

"No. I knew you'd remember. Oh, Custis — I've missed your letters so much!"

"I can stand anything about this war," he said, "except not knowing about you. So tell me — quick — everything that's happened." Then both of them were talking, whispering words that tumbled over other words, hurrying to catch up on all they had missed as they sat cross-legged on the carpet, their hands tightly joined in Bekah's flowered lap.

"You haven't seen Buck, have you?"

He smiled at her innocence. "Honey, there must be thousands of your men out there, and Buck could be one of them, but no, I haven't seen him."

"What about Mason?"

"I've run across him a few times since he joined up,

79

but I worry about my little brother, Bekah. He's been wounded twice already. I wish I could keep close to him, keep an eye on him."

"What has it been like for you, Custis, the past two years?"

"At first it was exciting. That's when we all thought it would be over in a minute, and we couldn't wait to get into a fight. And the ladies made us beautiful silk flags, and stuffed us full of pies and cakes, and sent us off like heroes, almost kissed to death."

"And now?"

He sighed. "It's different. Mostly boring. The real fighting only comes along from time to time, and the rest is marching and drilling and waiting. There's a heap of waiting, Bekah, and I never was too happy doing that. There's mud, and being too cold in winter and too hot in summer, and never having enough to eat, and settling down in one place and being told to move on somewhere else. There's dirt and sickness, and worst of all, the graybacks."

"Graybacks?"

He pinched an invisible thing between his thumb and finger.

"You mean *lice?*"

He laughed at the look on her face. "Mainly, though," he said, "it's just missing things. Like good coffee, and soft bread and" — he touched a strand of her hair — "the comfort of having womenfolk around."

"Are you ever afraid, Custis?"

"No, I don't believe I am. I'll come out of this all right. But Mason . . . he was always afraid when we were boys, thinking there were monsters under the bed and hiding in closets. He was scared of the dark. He had terrible nightmares."

"Today was like a nightmare," she told him. "Leander and I went out to Seminary Ridge to see what was going on, and suddenly shells were blowing up around us, and men were limping in from the fields all smashed and bleeding."

"But what did you expect?"

"I didn't expect it to be real. And it was!"

"You saw one ugly little corner of it, Bekah. I've seen the whole thing over and over, and believe me, it's worse than anything you can imagine. Yet sometimes . . . and I wouldn't tell this to anyone but you . . . there's a kind of crazy . . ." he paused, searching for the right word, "*joy* to it. Stonewall loved it too, when we had them on the run. You could see it in those eyes of his . . . the way he drove us . . . men excited and screaming and the colors flashing and the sound of bugles and the bands playing! And you're almost there, you've almost won, you can't be licked because your men are smarter and faster and better than anyone else. . . . That's how it is sometimes. There is that joy."

He looked as if what he had said surprised him. "Maybe that's why General Lee said that queer thing after we won at Fredericksburg. That it was a good thing that war was so terrible, or else we should grow too fond of it. Now I know what he meant."

"You think you'll win here too, don't you?"

"Yes, we'll win. The Lord is with us, Bekah. He wants the South to be free."

She felt a distance grow between them. "Custis, you are so wrong!" She pulled her hands away. "The Lord isn't on the side of slavery and rebellion. Those are evil things. Those things are an *abomination!* How can you be so blind?"

He got to his feet. "Let's not argue about it. I didn't mean to spoil things between us. We don't have much time. . . . I have to get back to Culp's Hill. By the way," he said, "Wes Culp's a friend of mine. He's in my company."

Her eyes sparkled angrily in the moonlight. "Wes Culp is a traitor to his family and to this town!"

"He's no more a traitor than I am! He's fighting for what he believes in, same as me!"

"But you believe in the wrong things!"

Unhappily they faced each other. "Bekah," Custis whispered. "If you only knew how tired I am."

Her anger had flashed, and was gone. "I wish you could stay here with us, and let the war move on someplace else."

"So do I." He took her face in his hands. "I came here to tell you something, Bekah. Maybe I shouldn't feel for you the way I do . . . us being cousins and all . . . but I do, and it's the best part of being alive. I love you, Bekah. That's what I had to tell you."

It was so unexpected, what he had said, so large and strange, and yet it was something she had always known. There was no quarrel between them now —

she felt as he did. She put her arms around him, and lifted her face, and he kissed her, not in the old way she remembered, a kiss that skidded past her cheek and slid away, but with his mouth on hers and a trembling in his hands. There was an asking and a giving in his touch, and she never wanted it to end. When it did, she asked, "Custis ... will I see you again?"

"I'm coming back, no matter what happens," he promised. "We'll settle things between us."

"Yes!" She hugged him hard, and kissed him again, feeling the new excitement flare between them. "Custis, I love you, too!"

July 2

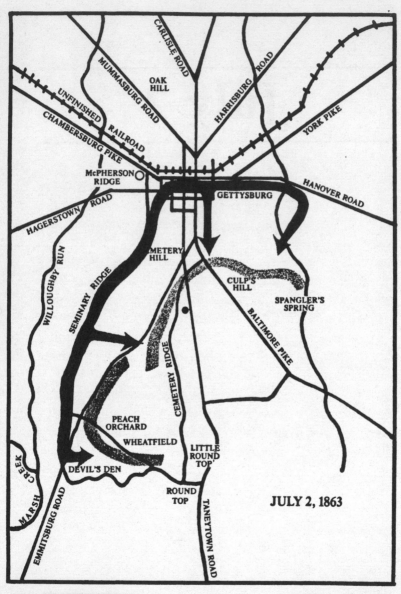

CARLISLE ROAD

MUMMASBURG ROAD

OAK HILL

HARRISBURG ROAD

UNFINISHED RAILROAD

CHAMBERSBURG PIKE

YORK PIKE

McPHERSON RIDGE

GETTYSBURG

HANOVER ROAD

HAGERSTOWN ROAD

WILLOUGHBY RUN

SEMINARY RIDGE

METERY HILL

CULP'S HILL

SPANGLER'S SPRING

BALTIMORE PIKE

CEMETERY RIDGE

PEACH ORCHARD

WHEATFIELD

LITTLE ROUND TOP

MARSH CREEK

EMMITSBURG ROAD

DEVIL'S DEN

ROUND TOP

TANEYTOWN ROAD

JULY 2, 1863

UNION

CONFEDERATE

● MEADE'S HEADQUARTERS

○ LEE'S HEADQUARTERS

12

IT WAS AFTER MIDNIGHT WHEN MEADE ARRIVED
from Taneytown. Hancock, the commander of the
Second Corps, had recommended that the army
make a stand along the fishhook of land south of
Gettysburg, and Meade, inspecting the lines during
the bright moonlit hours before dawn, agreed. By
morning most of the men would be up, except for
Sedgwick's Sixth Corps, now embarked on a thirty-
six-mile march. It would probably not arrive much
sooner than midday, but when it did, about ninety
thousand men would be in place.

At dawn the general, with field glasses screwed to
his eyes, was even more satisfied by what he saw.
Ahead of him a vast battlefield floated up out of the
morning fog: orchards and cultivated fields, neat
fences, a few small farmhouses. Now he could clearly
see the advantages of their position. The Federal line
was more elevated; his artillery would have more
range and power, and it would be easier for him to
move segments of the army back and forth than it
would be for Lee, whose troops would be stretched
thinner and farther than his own.

"Coffee, sir?" A wan aide with drooping eyes offered him a metal cup and dared to suggest, "You really ought to try and get some sleep."

"Get some yourself, if you need it."

The aide withdrew, hurt that his intentions had been misunderstood. He thought how rumpled and haggard the general looked, how irritable and fussy and hot-tempered the man could be. He decided against suggesting a wash and a change of clothes at headquarters. Obviously the commander of the Union army had more important matters on his mind.

Revived by the cool morning air, Meade gulped the hot, sweet coffee, and continued his survey. The fishhook image, which had snagged his inner vision in the night, was now exposed in the early light. The tip of the hook, at Culp's Hill, was occupied by Slocum's men, with the remnants of the First Corps strung out along the low saddle of land that joined Culp's Hill to Cemetery Hill. Here, what was left of Howard's battered Eleventh was protected by a heavy crescent of artillery. Then the hook bent, the shank running out along the ridge, with Hancock's reliable Second Corps in position and linking with Sickles's Third, which extended out in the direction of the two wooded knolls that anchored the extreme left. It crossed Meade's mind that if Lee managed to slide men in around the Round Tops and come in on the rear, it would be a serious problem. Sickles, posted at a vulnerable spot, must be trusted to prevent that from happening.

Too bad he didn't think much of Dan Sickles. The man was a murderer and a politician, a deadly combination, and Meade intended to keep a close eye on him.

Soldiers were stirring, yawning and rising, going about their early morning duties. Meade didn't notice them glancing at him out of the corners of their eyes; his mind was preoccupied. But as the smell of frying salt pork drifted greasily through the air he thought for the first time in hours of food.

Private Charlie Payne, carrying water back to his company, watched the new commander walk briskly toward the Union headquarters in the tiny Leister farmhouse beyond the ridge. "George!"

His friend lurched ahead, water splashing from two heavy pails.

"Did you see him?"

"See who?" Dawson stumbled, spilled more water, swore.

"General Meade!"

"I didn't notice."

"Wasn't much *to* notice," Charlie grumbled. He was disappointed. At least McClellan and Burnside and Fighting Joe Hooker had looked like men in charge. This one, with his wrinkled neck and cranky eyes—Charlie had to smile a little—looked more like a snapping turtle about to bite down hard.

At dawn Buck was rousted from a dark, safe cave of sleep and ordered to move. The men, who had marched twenty-five miles on the previous day, were thick-footed, half-dreaming. Sometimes when they halted for one reason or another the soldiers would sink into the deep, wet grass beside the road and nod off again, until some angry, shouting officer on horseback would crash through the fog and prod the groggy men back to their feet.

"Do you know where we are, Tully?" Even in a place filmed with mist, Buck was sure of himself. "We're coming up behind Cemetery Ridge."

Tully plodded ahead, his eyes remote, and Buck thought *I've brought him this far . . . just a little way to go.*

The morning sun, gliding up a pale blue summer sky, pulled off the last of the milky vapor and revealed the land. Buck felt a happy leap of pride. He was home. He knew these zigzag fences, the wheat- and cornfields, the contour and texture of the meadows bright with wildflowers. Shining wings careened overhead, and he recognized the pattern of each flight, each individual birdsong.

"Hell, this ain't no day to fight," Jesse Flynn said. "This here's a strawberry social sort of day. A day for lemonade."

"Why don't you mention it to General Meade," Buck suggested with a slow smile. "See if he'll rearrange his plans."

"Maybe we'll celebrate the Fourth of July here," Jesse said. "Maybe you'll introduce me to that pretty girl you carry around in your knapsack."

Buck wished he hadn't shown him the daguerreotype of Bekah. He hated it when the soldier asked to see it, sat staring at it, touching it with his thick, dirty fingers. "That girl's too young to care anything about men," he said.

"How old is she?"

"Not sixteen yet."

"My sister was married and had a baby in her lap before she was sixteen," Jesse said.

It disgusted Buck to think of such a thing. Bekah was a child. The last time he had seen her she'd been hanging upended from a branch, the ruffles of her petticoat cascading as she swung by her knees, grinning at him upside down, her big dark eyes like polka dots.

Hundreds of soldiers were massed behind the artillery parked ahead of them, with hundreds more pressing in from behind.

"Where do you suppose them rebels are?" Flynn wanted to know.

"Over on the other ridge." Buck, who always kept his ears open for useful information, had heard the officers talking. "Near the Lutheran Seminary."

"That don't sound fair. That means they got the Lord on their side this time."

Buck was glad that the Army of Northern Virginia was faceless, out of sight. It was easier to hate men you couldn't see. When a rebel picket hollered, "Why don't you-uns come over and fight we-uns? We want yer to," it was easy to believe he was meaner and more ignorant than a Northern man, and yet Buck knew that really wasn't true. Often there was joking and friendly conversations. Once, on duty on the Rappahannock, he had sent newspapers skidding across the water on a little raft, in exchange for some mellow Virginia tobacco; after dark some of his company had swum across and played cards with the Southern men.

Custis and Mason could be somewhere nearby. They had all wrestled together as youngsters, laughing and panting and sometimes crying with rage as they tried to pin each other to the ground, but he could never think of either of them as his enemy. Stories were always circulating in the army of fathers against sons, brothers against brothers, kin meeting kin in battle. Or men from the same family enlisting together, fighting and dying together. He hoped he would never see his cousins on the field.

He chewed hard crackers as the troops waited for the Sixth Corps to arrive and made sure Tully put some into his belly, too, though he knew his friend didn't care much about eating anymore. Again the Fifth Corps was ordered to move. This time Syke's men halted at a stream near a mill.

Buck said, "We used to come here a long time ago, remember?"

Tully stared at the green-white water spinning over the revolving steps of the wheel. It seemed to fascinate him as it had when he was a boy.

They were formed in columns by division and ordered to rest. There was the sound of skirmishing in the distance. Soon they would be part of the thing they had pushed so hard to reach. It was time to think of what lay ahead.

Jesse said hoarsely, "I've done bad things, Buck . . .

you know I have." He reached into his pocket and took out a tattered pack of playing cards. "Do you want these?"

Buck shook his head. "Throw them away if it will make you feel better."

Flynn sat, clutching the cards to his chest, trying to make up his mind. Gambling was sinful, and if a man was killed he wouldn't want the evidence on him when he reached the Heavenly Gates. Yet these were lucky cards, carefully marked. Finally he stuffed them back into his pocket. Nearby a chaplain was conducting a service for a huddle of solemn men, their voices a monotone of prayer. Buck pulled his own testament out of his uniform. His mother had made him memorize verses from it when he was a boy. It was at times like this that most men looked for comfort, for small hopeful signs. He let the book flop open, then he looked down and read some of the tiny printed words. *The Lord shall preserve thee from evil; He shall preserve thy soul.* Even though he wasn't superstitious, he could not help feeling cheered. Tully sat staring at his hands, knotted tensely together, and Buck wondered if he was thinking of Manassas, the skeleton finger pointing.

13

GENERAL LEE HAD HOPED TO TAKE CULP'S HILL FIRST
thing in the morning, but at dawn, when it was discovered to be occupied by Union troops, it seemed
wiser to hit both enemy flanks at the same time, and
as soon as possible. A. P. Hill's men, tired from their
work on the previous day, would concentrate on the
center of the line. Yet nothing went according to
plan, and as the bright morning dwindled away into
the soft, warm core of afternoon, only two of Longstreet's divisions were in place.

"I never like to go into battle with one boot off,"
Old Pete said as he sat and idly whittled, waiting for
the third division to arrive. Some of the high-ranking
officers murmured that he might be stalling because
he was so stubbornly opposed to Lee's strategy, but in
the meantime the infantry found it pleasant to rest
and smoke.

"Reckon it's worth a fight now and then just to get
a bellyfull." A private, gulping down the last of the
hardtack and salt pork he had robbed from the hav-
ersack of a dead Union soldier, sighed with satisfaction. Then, reaching into the bowl of his hat, he
dropped ripe cherries, one by one, into his open
mouth.

At three o'clock word came that Pickett would be

delayed until the following day. One boot or not, Longstreet knew he must go into battle with the men he had on hand.

A mile away on Cemetery Ridge, General Daniel Sickles had come to pester his superior, George Meade, and to explain how unhappy he was with the placement of his Third Corps out by the Round Tops.

"My orders were clear, weren't they?" Irritable from his sleepless night, Meade peered at the officer, whom he neither liked nor respected, with popping bloodshot eyes. "We need you there."

"The position is too flat!" Sickles was insistent. "The artillery is masked by the woods, and we can't see a damned thing!" Just ahead, however, about a half mile west along the Emmitsburg Road at a peach orchard, the land was slightly elevated. All Sickles wanted was permission to remove his men from where they were and put them on the higher ground where they ought to be before the enemy got there first.

Meade was annoyed. He was too busy to check the situation for himself, and yet he wasn't willing to trust the judgment of a man who wasn't even an army regular, a man who had won his stars through political connections. Sickles was tarnished, notorious, undisciplined. He'd been a congressman before the war, but had been cut from Washington social circles when he had shot his young wife's lover, Barton Keyes, the grandson of the man who had composed the national anthem. Sickles had pleaded temporary insanity and been acquitted, but some people felt that even worse than the murder was Sickles's shocking lack of taste in taking his wife back.

Anxious to get him out of the way, Meade hailed Henry Hunt, his chief of artillery, who was passing by on a hurried mission of his own. "Go and see what he's talking about, and report back to me!"

A short time later, when he had looked the situation over, Hunt told Sickles that he could see what he wanted to do and why. "But if you move the Corps out to the Emmitsburg Road you're going to leave a gap back here that will have to be plugged with some of the reserves. So it's not up to me to make that kind of decision."

"You can at least recommend it, can't you?" The general tugged at the collar of his uniform with quick, sharp jerks. "I've already sent Berdan out there with his sharpshooters, and they ran into rows of rebels getting ready to move in on my left. If we stay here we're sitting ducks."

Hunt wished that the excited man would calm down, that the matter was settled. He was anxious to get back to his artillery. "Look, I'll talk to General Meade and get back to you just as soon as I can."

All day the Union troops, massed along the shank of land south of town, had waited in hot sunshine for something to happen. Around noon there had been a brief fierce flurry of firing off near Seminary Ridge, and reports had come back that Berdan's men had uncovered a suspicious movement there, but except for light skirmishing and an occasional thump of artillery, nothing much had happened since. Then, midafternoon, the bright clear sound of trumpets lifted in the air.

"Take a look — over there!" Charlie Payne leaped to the top of the low stone wall ahead of him, and pointed to the slope that flattened out toward the Round Tops. "There goes the Third Corps! Now where do you suppose it's going *to?*"

From their position along the ridge, the men of the Second Corps could hear faint shouts, see skirmishers lightly feeling the advance as thousands in battle formation swept forward, horsedrawn guns and caissons bumping after in the rear.

"I reckon they've just gone down to pick some peaches." Unlike Charlie, who was high-strung and excitable, George Dawson was easy and relaxed. "But, hell . . . peaches ain't even ripe yet."

A lieutenant laughed, and spat tobacco juice on the ground. "Neither is Sickles."

Soldiers were being aligned along the dusty Emmitsburg Road, sent into Sherfy's orchard, and angled into the vicinity of Devil's Den. Charlie thought there was something grand and powerful about the spectacle of ten thousand infantrymen, strokes of blue planted among leafgreen and wheatyellow, bayonets sharp as needles piercing the golden afternoon.

"He done it perfect, didn't he!" George had a slow, kind face and round, sleepy eyes. He took off his forage cap and scratched his dirty ragged curls. " 'Cept for one little thing." He gestured in the direction of the rock-strewn area that lay beneath the anchoring hills. "Looks to me as if Sickles has run out of men."

From their elevated position they could see the obvious flaw in the operation. "Maybe they'll send in some of the reserves," Charlie said hopefully.

"They'd better hurry then, if they're thinking of it," the lieutenant said. "And I don't believe there's anyone up there, either." He blinked, straining to catch a glimpse of Union guns on Little Round Top.

"Signal officers. . . ." Charlie had glimpsed a wig-wag of flags near the summit of the hill.

"Better be more'n signal officers," George said. "Those rebels crawl up there . . . why, they'll nail this whole line shut tighter'n a coffin lid."

His men had barely been smoothed into place when Sickles received an order to attend a council of war. He sent his excuses off to Meade, but another messenger galloped back almost immediately with a demand that he come at once. The officer fumed. Enemy guns were warming up already, and it seemed ridiculous that he must obey at such a time. As he reached headquarters a noisy din was rising in the southwest, and smoke was puffing upward into the cloudless sky.

"Don't bother!" Meade stood in the doorway of the Leister house, angrily flapping his hands, telling him not to get off his horse. Sickles thought that he looked like a flustered housewife shooing geese. "I'm coming with you!"

Together they galloped back along the slope. Enemy artillery was pounding in, and Meade saw thick gray waves of infantry cresting Seminary Ridge, spilling down into the woods southwest of the peach orchard. He was astounded. The Third Corps was now open to attack on three sides, the whole Federal line was threatened, and his sturdy defensive fishhook had been snapped.

"Now you can see what I mean by superior ground." Sickles, with thousands of good men in danger, was quite unaware of what he had done.

A shell exploded in the road ahead of them. Meade's horse, Old Baldy, shuddered in fright. With his popping eyes and pursed lips the general looked as if he might explode himself. Sickles said hastily, "Of course if you *object* to the new disposition. . . ."

Meade wheeled toward him, his sallow face convulsed with mottled color. "I *do* object, sir! Vehemently! Both your flanks are in the air! *You have broken our line of defense!*"

Another shell screeched past and burst. Old Baldy reared in terror, and the general struggled to control him.

"Then we'll return to the old position at once," Sickles said sulkily, "if that's what you have decided."

"It's too late, General! The enemy has decided for us!" Meade started away, calling back, "You must do what you can! I'll send you support!"

It had seemed to Sickles that things had gone so smoothly and so well, and now he saw his plan had tugged loose like a sheet in the wind and was sailing out of control.

McLaws, steady and reliable, had gone about the business of shaking men from his division out along the ridge, but John Hood, who had reconnoitered on his own, sent a staff officer to General Longstreet with a bright suggestion. His Texas scouts had run into an advanced line of battle near an orchard, seen the main line of the enemy massed heavily along the opposite ridge, and discovered that the stony land that lay in front of the two rocky hills was a formidable barrier. How much simpler it would be, he suggested, to slide eastward, circle the knolls, and move in on the Federal rear, where the army trains and artillery were parked, exposed and vulnerable to attack.

What Hood wanted to do was exactly what Longstreet had already tried out on Lee, and he had had his answer to that more than once. Longstreet's reply was "General Lee's orders are to attack up the Emmitsburg Road."

It was the first, the only time in Hood's career that he had ever balked at going into battle. He tried to make his objections even clearer by sending another officer to Longstreet. The answer was brief. "General Lee's orders are to attack up the Emmitsburg Road."

Hood's third message invited his superior to come and look the situation over for himself.

"General Lee's orders are to attack up the Emmitsburg Road."

All right then. Frustrated, Hood stared across the valley. Timber had been cut, exposing the western slope of the smaller hill, and he was almost certain there were no Union soldiers there yet. He was sure he could guide his men around successfully and pounce on the rear of the enemy without too much risk. Yet he also knew it would be easier to move those little mountains than to persuade Old Pete to change his mind.

Longstreet had arrived on horseback. Cool professionals, their eyes met briefly.

"General Lee isn't feeling well today. A touch of the Old Soldier's Disease. . . ." Hood sensed that Longstreet was giving him this information as some sort of explanation. "You know we must obey his orders."

Hood nodded. Reluctantly he gave the command. Men advanced to the lip of the ridge and poured down into the sunlit valley. Twenty minutes later the general was carried from the field with a paralyzing arm wound, and bitter regrets that would last him his lifetime.

Sixty Confederate guns had opened fire, followed by a hard-driving infantry attack. In the new position the Third Corps was overwhelmed by a vicious assault as shot and shell ripped through the tidy rows of the peach orchard, knocking off branches, shredding men to pieces. The battle had become a wind-whipped fire that raged this way and that, leaping fences, flickering around a farmhouse and its out-buildings, dying away and flashing back to blazing life as ground was won and lost and won again.

"We ought to be down there." Private George Dawson looked down calmly at bits of blue and dun-colored daubs kneeling and firing, running from tree to tree in a thickening haze. Smoke swelled and billowed skyward, shifting at times to reveal splintered caissons, torn and dying horses struggling on the ground, crippled soldiers hobbling out along the road. "Hancock should send us in to help."

"It's their fight now." Charlie Payne was relieved that he was high on the ridge, behind the sheltering stone wall. "But if they give way, it'll be our fight, too." He prayed for Sickles's men to hang on.

Far below hundreds plunged into a wheatfield, senses flayed open, blood pumping, sweat pouring down their powder-blackened faces, their breath whining hard and fast through mouths and noses. Minie balls spanged and hummed among running, spinning, falling shapes; crouching men groped for cartridges, tore the paper twists with their teeth, mechanically performed the ten separate motions necessary to reload the heated guns. A Union private absently slapped his chest, saw blood gush out between his fingers, wondered if death could be such a tiny sting, and toppled sideways. An artilleryman saw his boot land yards away, discovered that his foot was in it.

"Quick! Over here!" Wounded, Dan Sickles called

for help. "Get something to tie this thing up before I bleed to death!"

He was carried off the field, a cigar clamped hard between his teeth. Half an hour later his shattered leg had been removed.

14

G. K. WARREN, CHIEF ENGINEER OF THE UNION ARMY, had been sent by Meade to investigate the left. From the summit of Little Round Top he looked down into a smashed orchard and the smoking whirlpool of a wheatfield. Shouts rose, and faint defiant yells; he heard the crackle of muskets, the boom and thud of artillery. Sickles's salient had been hit hard on three sides and was badly damaged, and Warren did not see how it could hold out much longer. He saw something else that alarmed him. Quick gray-brown shapes were gliding into the jagged wasteland near the bottom of the hill, taking shelter behind immense lopsided boulders, squeezing into the cracks and crannies of Devil's Den. Rebel sharpshooters. The enemy had already overlapped Sickles's crumbling flank and was sweeping ahead in Warren's direction.

Big Round Top, farther to the south, was higher, but so densely wooded that it would be almost impossible to get artillery up there. *This* was the vital spot, then; Little Round Top was the key to the field, and for some unfathomable reason it was completely undefended. Except for a signal officer, hastily packing up to leave, the engineer was alone on the hill. If the Confederates got there and managed to get their guns to the top, they would be able to enfilade the whole Union line. The battle would be over.

"Don't go!" He shouted to the signal officer. "Keep waving those flags — let them think there's somebody up here!"

The man nodded, and began to jerk the flags back and forth. Flushed with heat and a terrible anxiety, Warren picked his way down the hill, loose pebbles scattering from under his horse's hooves. Emerging from the brush at the bottom of the hill, he galloped off to look for help.

He was in luck. He ran into Vincent's brigade, quick-stepping along the road toward the wheatfield, and managed to divert it. Men were sent scrambling up the steep face of Little Round Top. A battery of artillery followed, the gun crew grunting and straining as they dragged and pushed the heavy weapons up over the rocks.

"We could find our way up here blindfolded, couldn't we, Tull?"

Smoky sunlight drifted down through the treetops, splattering across the lichen-crusted boulders. The sound of the battle behind the hill was blurred. Buck grabbed a scrub oak and pulled himself higher, exhilarated to be in a place he knew so well. Below him Tully climbed slowly, his face hidden by the peak of his forage cap. Buck wanted to grab him, shake him, force him to hurry. Instead he paused to catch his breath, said, "Custis and Bekah and I camped out here one night." It seemed a very long time ago. He remembered the black sky, crowded with stars, curving over him and how he had felt his life waited for him beyond the darkness, a distant adventure as mysterious and remote as the long streaks of light falling overhead, dying in the summer night.

They had reached the top. To his right, through a screen of pine branches, Buck caught his first glimpse of Gettysburg. How close it was, only a battle-span away. To the west he heard the sharp metallic crack of rifle fire, the moan of missiles gliding in through the mangled branches of Sherfy's peach orchard below, where he and the town boys had been drawn like flies each year when the fruit was ripe. Bodies like torn rags were draped beneath the damaged trees, hung over fence rails, scattered out along the Emmitsburg Road. Shells burst violently across a smudged wheatfield, dirty smoke masking the shapes of running men, the blunt brutal noses of the cannons.

"On the right by file into line!" Urgently Colonel Strong Vincent lapped his four regiments into a quarter-circle around the southwest shoulder of the hill. "This is the end of the line!" he called to Chamberlain, the commander of the 20th Maine. "You understand! You must hold this ground at all costs!"

Chamberlain nodded. His unit, hunched well below the crest, had only a few sparse oaks in front of it, too small to offer much protection, and his men were busily making breastworks out of logs and fallen branches, taking shelter.

At all costs. Buck felt a queer shock. He opened his canteen, gulped the warm water Eighty, maybe ninety thousand men stretched in a wide blue band all the way to Culp's Hill two or three miles away, and yet here on the summit of Little Round Top, almost by accident, one brigade was holding down the entire line. The place should have been defended like a fortress, buckled around with iron, bristling with big guns. *But instead there's only us,* he thought, *one battery of artillery.* If they let go then the whole weight of the Union army might topple over in one devastating landslide. He didn't want to think about that. Buck licked his dry lips, feeling thirsty again.

Around him soldiers were digging in, ducking behind rocks and trees. His regiment was linked to the Maine men at the far left, with the New Yorkers scuttling into position to the right. A lucky sign. The 44th was their regimental twin; they had fought side by side with them in every battle. Where the hill curved around to the north, Michiganders gazed across Plum Run into a stretch of stony rubble where minie balls were already ricocheting in among the rocks.

Tully. He stood, rifle dangling, staring off into the distance. That familiar absence in his face, as if he had sidestepped out of time and was back in some friendly zone of childhood. He had played on this hill when he was a boy, rolled down these slopes pretending to be dead, sprung back to life with a laugh.

Buck saw that Tully wasn't going to fight. Knowing it filled him with a helpless anger. Earlier they had been read an order handed down from General Meade. "Corps and other commanders are authorized to order instant death to any soldier who fails to do his duty at this hour." His friend hadn't listened, didn't care. Why did *he* always have to be responsible, especially now with his own life in danger? He grabbed the other musket, loaded it, rammed the Enfield hard against Tully's chest. "When they get here, you'd better shoot, damn you!" he hissed. "You hear me? You *shoot!*"

Ahead, down the hillside, was a wide granite slab, creased at the top, bushes thick and springy around its base. Buck pushed Tully toward it and shoved him down. There was no resistance; it was a straw man that he pressed flat against the stone. "You stay there!" His voice was hoarse with strain. "And don't move!" He knew he wasn't getting through. Tully just wasn't going to let himself be there. Buck hunkered, sweat rolling down his face, stinging his eyes, soaking through the heavy wool of his uniform. He said quietly, "Listen . . . if you can't do it, if you can't shoot . . . then play dead." He waited, wanting to make sure that he was understood. "When they get here you just play dead, Tull . . . the way we used to, remember? I'll try and cover you."

Up the hill, not far away, he found a stump, thick

and wide and rotten. Ants flowed in and out. A short distance behind him Jesse Flynn was crouched behind a rock.

"I keep thinking of lemonade," he said. "Ice-cold lemonade."

"When it's over," Buck said, "maybe we can go home, and Bekah can fix some for us."

"With the rinds floating in it?"

"That's how she makes it."

Flynn smiled, wiped his forehead with his sleeve. "I look forward to it." He winked. "And to meeting her."

There was the leaden thug of muskets being loaded along the line, the clash and clang of rammers. Buck reached for a cartridge, ripped off the paper with his teeth. A soldier ought to have good front teeth, but he'd seen some with poor ones or none at all, and wondered how they stayed alive. Once in a battle on the Peninsula he'd been too excited and kept on loading the musket, jamming the muzzle, forgetting to fire. How dumb and green he had been in those days.

Morrill's Company dropped down the slope, men moving warily, rifles held high as the skirmishers disappeared among the foliage at the bottom of the hill. Buck tucked himself in small behind the stump, feeling the tension crackling among the soldiers waiting near the top. Minutes later a high, wild scream rose from the valley to the south. About a quarter of a mile away three lines of enemy troops were plunging forward, sunlight glancing off their bayonets.

"Come to the ready . . . take good aim. . . ."

Men in sun-bleached gray and yellow-brown swept in closer, then they were rising up the hill, growing fierce faces and terrible eyes and wide-open yelling mouths that trailed the high-pitched rebel wail. *Indians,* Buck thought, *that's where they get it from.* He and his friends had made that same sound as boys, whapping their hands across their lips.

He waited, coolly chose, aimed and fired, watched a long body dance through space and crash, dirt-colored, on the ground. His eyes flicked to Tully, curled motionless behind the rock. *Stay there. Don't move.* With furious rhythm Buck knelt, reloaded, aimed low and fired again as hundreds of bodies lapped upward in a thick, rising tide. Buck thought, *Outnumbered — so few of us and all of them.* Minie balls slashed through branches, riddled tree trunks, sizzled against stone, and then Union cannister was ripping into the advance, whirling iron balls spraying the enemy like a deadly hail, tearing huge holes in the ranks. Men from Texas and Alabama were going down, but others were pushing up from behind, desperation a hot, driving force. *If they reach here they've got us, they've won.* Buck ripped paper viciously, jammed in a cartridge, sensed a sudden wavering hesitation below and saw the wave break at last, curling back and ebbing swiftly down the slope, leaving dozens of bodies beached against the hillside, some limp, some rolling and twisting in their pain. Jesse Flynn fired steadily into the retreating mass, cursing, his voice high and shrill. "They're going — going — !"

"They'll be back," Buck muttered. They always came back. Quickly he glanced around. Men from the Ambulance Corps were dragging the wounded to the rear. An excited drummer boy, no more than fourteen or fifteen, had wriggled into a place along the line and was loading a rifle; a musician snatched up a musket from a fallen man; a color bearer jammed a staff into a crevice in the rocks and freed his hands to fire. Colonel Vincent, dark and erect, stood high on a boulder shouting orders, but Buck couldn't hear him above the uproar.

Flynn shrieked, "Here they come — here they come!" There was a long, timeless interval as a fresh assault screamed up the hillside, fell back, climbed higher, clawed closer to the top. Jesse Flynn sucked in breath, pitched headlong, flopped once, and lay still with open, staring eyes. A running figure leaped through a haze of smoke, saw Tully, raised a bayonet. Buck fired. The rebel toppled, a sprawled hand dripping red across the body curled against the rock.

Once again swift, darting forms were slipping back, dropping away. Buck, watching through an eerie reddish glow, wondered if something had broken in his head, if his brain were filling up with blood. Energy was leaking out along the line, the men gasping and grunting with exhaustion. His fingers fumbled thickly as he reached for ammunition. Sixty rounds at the start, and now he was almost out.

Something odd was happening below. He glimpsed an enemy column drifting away to the left,

110

then lost it beneath the trees. Why over there? No time to think — he needed cartridges. On his belly Buck twisted down across a scattered trail of bloodied playing cards toward a dead body. A bad hand for Jesse Flynn. He didn't look into his face. The cartridge box was warm and sticky. Buck took what there was, shimmied back to his shelter behind the rotten stump.

A curious maneuver was taking place among the men from Maine. Swiftly, in one fluid motion, Chamberlain had bent back his left into a right angle to form a solid line; soldiers were scrambling to hide themselves among the rocks and underbrush as the right dodged and shifted sideways, hurrying to form a single rank that would cover the original front.

"Quick! This way — hurry. Over here. . . ." Now the 83rd was being moved, sent sliding over to help fill in the gaps. The gray column that had disappeared under the trees, climbing the hill without being seen, had expected to fall in on an unguarded left. Now as the Alabamans charged out of hiding and into the open they met a fierce blast of resistance from Chamberlain's concealed, bent-back wing. With a roar the two forces smashed head-on, grappling in hand-to-hand combat. Men who had been lumberjacks swung their muskets like axes, slashing and chopping; bodies rolled over and over on the ground, furiously clenched, beating at each other with guns, fists, rocks, growling and snarling like dogs.

111

Charges, countercharges, furious bursts of action brawled up and down the slope in a reverberating, inhuman clash of sound.

"Quick! I need cartridges!" a soldier shouted to Buck.

"Can't! I'm out!"

"Ammunition! Ammunition!" There was an angry rising buzz all along the line as men groped among the fallen bodies in a frantic search. For Buck it was the most bitter moment he had ever experienced in battle. They had hung on, the frail fence of the brigade had held out the enemy, and at the critical moment there was nothing left to fight with. The next attack would crash over them, beginning the fatal downhill plunge that would sweep away the war.

"Fix bayonets!" Chamberlain's order shocked his men, silenced them. There was a blankness on their blackened faces, an incomprehension. Then, with a keen metallic rustling, they obeyed. The colors rose.

"Charge, bayonets! Charge!" A lieutenant leaped forward, followed by the color sergeant.

"Come on, boys!"

Incredulous, Buck watched the Maine regiment knife downhill in a great swinging thrust. Below, faces gaped upward, astonished, frozen into shapes of fear as the movement gained momentum, cut closer in a broad, glittering, scythe-like stroke. Then the rebels were turning, flying in panic, throwing away their weapons as they ran.

"Look — oh, look at 'em. I've never seen 'em skedaddle before!" crooned a happy voice behind Buck. "They're runnin' just like rabbits. Oh, that's a pretty sight!"

Far below gunfire sliced in obliquely from the left. Buck saw a row of muskets spaced along a low wall beneath the trees. He remembered Morrill's skirmishers, who had disappeared at the beginning of the fight. *They couldn't get back here. . . Must have been hiding there all the time. Their chance now. . . .*

Buck took a quick glance around. Blood splashed everywhere, puddles of it gleaming among the rocks. Colonel Vincent down, dozens of officers down, hundreds of men lying soaked and limp everywhere he looked. The cost had been terrible, but they had held Little Round Top, fastened down the drifting Union line. He had known they were good fighters all along, and given a chance they had proved it.

Soldiers were coming out from their shelters, running downhill, eager to get in on the rout.

"Prisoners! Let's get some prisoners!"

Then Buck was running too, shouting with joy, ignoring the sporadic fire still spattering in fitfully from the right. Something exploded viciously into his lower leg. The impact knocked him over, sent him rolling in the dirt, tore out his breath, floated him off into a calm of black.

15

WES CULP CHECKED HIS AMMUNITION AND RUBBED the stock of his gun with his sleeve. He was proud of his rifle, cut down to fit his size. His name was carved on it. "Cus, you look too happy to be sane."

"You think I'm happy about going up there?" Custis glanced briefly at Culp's Hill. "Well, I'm not. I never like looking up when I have to fight. That's what's wrong with this battle, Wes. For some reason we've got the wrong angle on it this time. Usually we've got the bluebellies squinting up at us."

Soldiers were stamping out the supper fires. Nearby a chaplain knelt among a circle of men, praying softly. Some sat alone with their testaments, lips moving silently as they repeated familiar passages. The old commander had been a strong one for religion, and Jackson's influence still lingered in the brigade.

Custis said, "I wish you had seen her, Wes. I mean the way Bekah stood up to me. She even threatened to blow off my head."

"Oh, touching," Wes said. "A charming girl."

"She is, though. Beautiful, too. I wish I could get back to town tonight."

"I have to go again when I can. I forgot to deliver that letter Jack Skelly gave me for his girl."

"Tomorrow," Custis decided. "We'll both go tomorrow."

"My sisters were real happy and surprised to see me," Wes said. "We didn't say much about the battle. We just talked about old times, old friends."

Custis was thinking of Bekah. It had been a strange day, waiting in the hot sun, wondering what was going to happen next. Nothing had. They had listened to the rumble in the distance, and reports had come in that there had been a big victory for them out along the ridge, but if that was true, then why was it so important to take Uncle Henry's hill all of a sudden?

He had written a letter, trying to scratch out in words the wonder he was feeling. He wanted to be with Bekah. He had been afraid to hold her, but she had put her arms around him, and when he had kissed her she had kissed him back, no starched embroidery or steel hoops between them, just her body warm and soft beneath her nightclothes.

He wished they would hurry up and climb the hill and take it, so he could go back and see her again, kiss her again.

"Bekah," the captain said. "Your name is Bekah, isn't it?"

"Yes." She came to the side of the bed, pleased that he was awake. "Is there anything you need?"

"Water, please. I'm thirsty."

She helped him drink. He looked feverish. His eyes were strange and bright.

"What day is this?"

"It's Thursday. The second of July."

"Do you know what's happening out there?"

"Nobody knows very much. The rebels have taken the town, and they act as if it's all going their way, but the battle isn't over yet."

It was almost seven o'clock in the evening, and the distant thunder that had rumbled out near the Round Tops had finally died away. The Weikert farm was close to there, and Bekah had been wondering about Tillie Pierce. Now a new disturbance had started up in the direction of Culp's Hill, and was growing louder. She had been thinking about Custis all day.

"There's no good news, then," said the captain.

"The Snyders have hidden their cow in the parlor." Bekah smiled. "I'll try and get some milk for you soon."

He smiled back. "Please don't bother. I know I've been a nuisance to you. I only came here because I'd seen too many field hospitals, and I was afraid I'd lose my arm."

"You were right to come. Dr. Horner took good care of you."

"Bekah ... I do have a favor to ask. Would you write a letter for me?"

"Of course I will. Your parents will be worrying about you."

"My parents are dead, but there is someone, a dear friend of mine ... I'm concerned about her. It's been so long since I've had word from her."

116

"I'll get some paper, and you can tell me what to write. As soon as the post office opens again, I'll mail it for you."

Later, as he slept, she read the letter over, curious about the woman who would receive it.

> My dear Anna:
>
> I am unable to write this letter for myself, but a kind young lady has consented to do it for me. By now you will have heard that a great battle is taking place at Gettysburg, although the outcome has not yet been decided. I am greatly worried, as the rebels have taken possession of the town, and boast that they have beaten us.
>
> Anna, I am wounded, although not too seriously. It has been some time since I have had any news of you. I hope you have not been ill. Please reassure me. If only this were the last battle of the war, and I could come to you and reassure myself.
>
> Your affectionate
> friend,
> Adam

She did not think she liked this woman who would not take a few minutes of her time to write to the man who loved her.

This must be hell, this stifling inferno of shrieks and sobs, this evil stench and mindless ranting.

"Mother? Mother! Mother, please pray for me...."

"Save me, Lord. Save me ... save me...."

Curses, thick, guttural, obscene. The reek of sweat

117

and urine. Shadowy figures passing. Hot fangs of pain gripped Buck's leg. A blurred figure swayed above him. "Hold on, son. It won't be long."

Had he groaned, or called for help? Buck's lips were swollen with thirst. "Water?"

"It's gone . . . we've sent for more. Hold on. . . ."

Not hell then, after all. Worse than that, Buck guessed — a field hospital, probably a barn. He felt the rough straw bunched under him. The floor, where he lay, was packed with bodies. Injured men drooped against the walls or squatted, staring dully into space. Some had bloody rags tied around their wounds; some cupped their faces despairingly in their hands. Voices prayed, babbled, bargained.

Winged insects fluttered softly around a smoking lantern. A surgeon with a knife held in his teeth waited as two assistants struggled with a man writhing on a wooden trestle. Finally, as one of the aides administered the chloroform, the man's arms relaxed and flopped limply to his sides. The surgeon pulled a dripping sponge from a bucket, swabbed, took the knife from his mouth, wiped it on his blood-smeared linen apron, and began to cut.

Buck felt an inner trembling, but he couldn't look away. There was the ghastly rasp of metal splintering bone. The doctor had a saw now, and his arm was moving back and forth across the makeshift table. *Please, no.* Buck's mind begged over and over. *Please, no.* He was shuddering uncontrollably, his teeth set hard against the sound. An object flashed, slapped wetly into a pile of amputated limbs heaped on the floor beneath the trestle.

Close to his ear a voice asked, "Danny?"

Buck turned his head, saw the slack stubbled face of an older man. His chest was black with blood, and soaked rags were stuffed into the gaping hole. "Danny? You'll take care of your mother?"

Buck knew that the man would die. Arms and legs could be treated, but severe wounds to head and chest and belly were set aside. There was never time to waste on men who weren't going to survive.

"Will you, Danny? Promise. . . ."

"Yes," Buck said. "I will."

The man sighed. "That cough troubles her. . . ."

"Yes."

"I'll be home before the baby comes, you tell her that."

"I will."

The man smiled. He seemed to feel no pain. "I always could depend on you, son."

Buck, with effort, answered, "Yes."

There was another patient on the table now, held down by the aides. It was a young boy hysterically crying, gulping his tears like a terrified child. The pungent smell, then silence.

"Danny?" A whisper.

"Shhhhh. . . ." Buck was too tired to talk. "I'm here. Just rest."

There was the friction of the metal saw.

A man needed two legs. For marching — why that

119

last day's tramp to Gettysburg had been at least twenty-five miles. Try hopping that on a wooden peg! For snowball fights in winter camp when the boredom set in, and soldiers whooped and played like youngsters in an innocent white warfare. Swimming! He thought of nude bodies ducking, splashing in the water, and a skinny rebel with all his ribs showing shouting across the glitter of the Rappahannock, "Ain't it a caution! You-uns look just like we-uns without yer britches!" Courting. He loved Mary Virginia, with her shining braids and vanilla fragrance, but she was older, and never would take him seriously. Imagine dancing on a wooden leg. What girl would want a crippled lover?

His leg was shredded pain. The surgeon was haggard, but he didn't have a cruel face. Maybe he would cut the agony away, and leave the limb intact. Surely he would, if Buck could explain how much he needed it.

The Lord shall preserve thee from evil. He shall preserve thy soul. But what about his leg!

Hands were raising him. He willed himself not to cry out, not to struggle. *Please, God,* he begged silently, *please, no.*

"Next!"

16

THE SECOND DAY OF JULY, SLOW TO IGNITE, HAD NOT burst into flames until late afternoon. Hours later, as a smoky dusk filled the acrid valley, pressed up against the ridges and thickened at the Round Tops, the day still smoldered fitfully, refusing to burn out. There were occasional dull rumblings, and spiteful bursts of firing from the Union left as the damaged armies slowly pulled themselves together, waiting for darkness to search for the wounded and hastily cover up some of the dead. But it was the Federal right that sparked and crackled now, where rifle fire flared like matches scratched against the fading light. On Cemetery Hill artillerymen stoked the big guns with a killing fire; on Culp's Hill a lone brigade watched a fresh attack blaze in from the northeast and wished that Slocum's men, who had left the entrenchments to help out Sickles hours before, would hurry back.

"Well, General Stuart . . . you are here at last."

The cavalry commander must have noticed the faint pucker of irony in the words, but Lee was not inclined to scold his officers, and Jeb Stuart did not really expect to be scolded. He was a good man who had made an unfortunate mistake, but he was sorry, and had arrived with his usual clink and sheen, plumed hat in hand, to say so. He was not allowed to do much more than that. The general heard what Stuart had to say, then nodded and dismissed him.

"I congratulate you, sir." Stuart got quickly to his feet, his cheerful smile gleaming through the handsome ruddy beard. "I hear you've won a great victory here this afternoon."

"I wish my information was as quick to arrive as yours." It was a mild rebuke, as far as Lee would go. "There's no victory yet. But the day isn't over, is it?"

He thought that Stuart left with a shade less jingle than he'd had when he arrived.

He needed to walk, to think. Alone, with his hands clasped behind his back, Lee strolled out along the ridge. It was early evening. Soldiers were munching on whatever was on hand for supper. As their commander passed they grew silent, and he was touched, as always, by that hushed respect. A boy boiling cornmeal, his back to the general, sang —

> Just before the battle, Mother,
> I was drinking mountain dew.
> When I saw the rebels marching
> To the rear I quickly flew.

He was shushed by a companion.

Lee thought of the men who had fought that afternoon. Hundreds dead, many lying with wounds festering in the trampled fields. Tragic. Tragic. All for a partial victory; a bloody patchwork of territory, the broken orchard and the ruined wheatfield. Some had made it as far as the ridge and had broken through the Union line, but there hadn't been support and the opportunity had been lost. An incredible effort had been made to capture the little mountain, but that had failed, too. Not a good day, not a good day at all. He had hoped to start early and attack both flanks, buckle *those people* in the middle, but instead of the smoothly coordinated strokes he had planned, the assault had been mainly a series of spasmodic punches, and in the long run they hadn't accomplished much. Maybe Ewell, the new corps commander, had been too timid, had felt Stonewall breathing over his shoulder. Maybe Longstreet, the seasoned one, had limped a bit more than was necessary in following orders. Maybe.

Or was it something in himself, not just the balky heart or the dysentery, but some warning stumble in his brain that meant he was too old for all of this.

He hoped not. He was good at it, and he liked to be successful. At times he wondered how he had come by this dark knack for war. Destiny, he guessed. God's will had always guided him, even when he had chosen his loyalty to Virginia over his allegiance to the country. He must live to see it through.

Something was happening on Cemetery Hill, flashing movement, streaks of fire, the crash and grumble of artillery. Good, that was good. Perhaps by dark Jubal Early's troops would accomplish what

Old Pete's had failed to do that afternoon: capture the higher ground and roll up the Union line.

Nobody noticed him. Most of the men were disabled, some limping two by two, some carried on litters, others using sticks or guns as crutches as they hobbled by. Tully moved stiffly among the shuffling mass, his eyes fixed on some distant point.

"Fresh milk! Fresh milk!" A fat-bellied farmer was peddling supplies.

"How much?"

"Dollar a quart."

Jeers, catcalls, oaths. "Robber! You know what you can do with it!"

"Take it or leave it. . . ."

Ambulances jolted past, the wounded groaning at every bump in the road. Sutler's carts, white canvas-topped supply wagons, officers on horseback impatient to push through, dazed stragglers dragging by on foot. Fence rails had been knocked down and set blazing, and the smell of frying pork hung in the air.

"Shoot me! Shoot me — please!" A hand caught hold of Tully's ankle, held him. He looked down into a grimy face, into the rolling eyes of the man pleading with him from the ditch. "I can't stand it no more — look!" He fumbled with his jacket, threw it open, but Tully refused to look at the horror that the soldier wanted him to see. He shook his ankle loose, felt the weak fingers slip away. Both sides of the road were smeared with the wounded. At dawn these meadows had threatened him with a sinister calm, but their writing motion terrified him now. All around him voices were calling out, begging for doctors, for food and water and whiskey, for mothers, fathers, wives, and children in a wild babble of misery.

Near a hospital tent Tully watched a musician take off his jacket and tuck it out of sight behind a box of supplies close to a great heap of amputated limbs. Then, rolling up his shirtsleeves, he ducked inside. Tully moved quickly. Moments later, buttoning on a tight coat trimmed with a lighter blue, he plunged into a field to begin his search. Nobody would question him. Once the bands stopped playing musicians were expected to double as medical aides.

"It's our turn now. . . . And here they come!"

Artilleryman Chauncy Sullivan stood by the brass Napoleon on Cemetery Hill and stared as neat gray columns poured out from Gettysburg into the outlying fields, muskets flashing in the stained twilight. "It's like watching a parade," he said. "Those Southern boys look almost too pretty to hit."

"You'd better stop admiring and start firing," grinned a veteran close to him, "or they'll be parading right over our heads."

Confederate guns erupted; Federal cannons exploded in reply, the long-range missiles streaking through the air and bursting, one after another, among the advancing troops. Then Union fire hosed in from the left, and Chauncy saw the perfect lines gape apart, crowds of men dissolving in thick piles of rising smoke. Yet others kept coming on; they reached the base of the hill and charged upward.

"Our boys are running!" Amazed, Chauncy watched the thin line of defense posted along the lower slope suddenly scatter. "Oh, those rotten cowards — the Eleventh is running *again!*"

Crews could no longer depress the big guns low enough to sweep the hillside, and orders came to cram in shrapnel, grape, and cannister.

"Fire by piece! Fire at will!"

The fierce shrieks rose higher, drew nearer. Louisiana Tigers poured over the banks of a ravine, hurtled a low wall, drove upward toward the crest of Cemetery Hill. If they reached the top, Chauncy knew, they could spill down across the Baltimore Pike beyond and wash up behind the Federal line. If that happened the day would flicker out in a humiliating defeat. But not without one last bitter fight.

As the enemy soldiers leaped in across the redoubts, the gunners met them with revolvers, rammers, handspikes, stones, and fists. Teeth clenched and faces contorted, whining in fury, the men grappled hand-to-hand, smashing, wounding, choking, killing. Thrown to the ground Chauncy Sullivan saw his sun streak down forever in a blaze of bayonet.

Nearby a Union battery swung sideways, firing double cannister into the rebel flank at almost point-blank range.

"Charge!" A great bullfrog command from Carroll, whose brigade had just arrived, sent blue bodies surging in upon the gray. In a roar of sound they were forcing the Tigers back down the slope, beating out the wavering screams, sending the survivors scattering off into the darkness.

It was over.

July 3

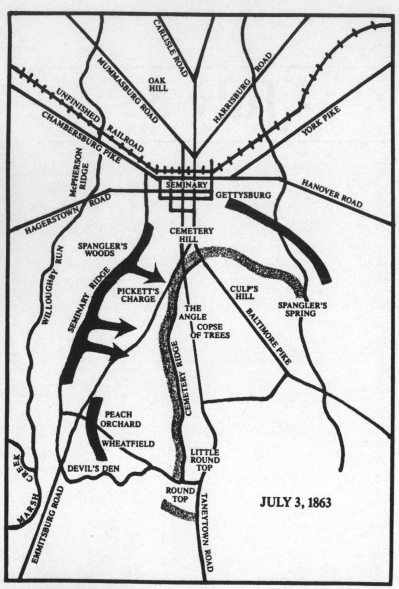

CARLISLE ROAD

MUMMASBURG ROAD

OAK HILL

HARRISBURG ROAD

UNFINISHED RAILROAD

CHAMBERSBURG PIKE

YORK PIKE

McPHERSON RIDGE

HANOVER ROAD

SEMINARY

GETTYSBURG

HAGERSTOWN ROAD

CEMETERY HILL

SPANGLER'S WOODS

WILLOUGHBY RUN

SEMINARY RIDGE

PICKETT'S CHARGE

CULP'S HILL

SPANGLER'S SPRING

THE ANGLE

COPSE OF TREES

BALTIMORE PIKE

CEMETERY RIDGE

PEACH ORCHARD

WHEATFIELD

LITTLE ROUND TOP

DEVIL'S DEN

JULY 3, 1863

ROUND TOP

CREEK

MARSH

EMMITSBURG ROAD

TANEYTOWN ROAD

UNION

CONFEDERATE

17

"WES?" THE WHISPER CAME OUT OF THE BLACKNESS. "Are you still there?"

·Quiet laughter. "Where did you think I was?"

"I don't know. Thought maybe you'd wandered off to see old Uncle Henry."

"Cus . . . are you crazy?"

There was a distant spatter of gunfire, faint, far-away shouts, then silence. "I thought this day would never end." Custis yawned. "Do you think it's really over?"

"Stop talking. Stop asking questions all the time. And get some sleep. We're not taking this hill to-night, that's for sure."

"I've never slept in a trench before. Have you?"

There was no answer.

It was after midnight. Since dusk Johnson's men had clung to the wooded slopes of Culp's Hill, at-tacking through thick underbrush, diving under logs, rolling under bushes, ducking from tree to tree and rock to rock, firing and reloading, then wriggling forward again. Four times they had almost made it to the top before they had been driven down again, forced to retreat. Custis had expected the uphill fight to be tough, had expected there would be heavy resistance from behind the sturdy Union breastworks, but what had surprised him most was finding the empty trenches dug in around the hillside.

"Wes . . . why do you suppose they dug these holes and then went off and left them?" He answered himself. "Yankee hospitality. They wanted us to feel at home."

Wes laughed. "I *am* at home. Remember?"

"I can't see a thing. Do you know where we are?"

"Far as I can figure it out, our rear ends are almost dragging on the Baltimore Pike. We're smack behind the whole Union army."

"We are?" Another gust of musketry faded off into a blank of silence. Custis whistled softly. "Does anyone else know it?"

"How would I know?"

"But if we're already in on their rear, shouldn't we be doing something about it?"

"Like what? You want me to stroll on over there and invite all those nice boys to surrender?"

"But we could take them by surprise."

"Custis." Wes Culp's voice was vague with weariness. "Stop asking things that I can't answer. Today is over. In a few hours the sun will be up, and we'll have a lot of work to do. Let me sleep."

"All right." There was a pause. "But when this is over, we'll go to town together, won't we?"

"Mmmmm."

"Wes? What if the men who left these trenches decide to come back?"

There was no reply.

On the battlefield nights and days became tangled, military routines intermingled. Sunlight could be a killing business, red with risk, or simply the marking of time behind the lines in dozing, eating, reading, praying. Darkness was sleep for weary men, or an edgy wakefulness for soldiers clinging to a hillside, surgeons in a midnight tent, or pickets on predawn duty. It might also cover secret movements, missions, meetings.

At the council of war at the cramped Union headquarters, a stub of candle had been stuck into a pool of melted wax on a tabletop. Cigar smoke curled around the little room. There was no disagreement among the officers wearing the dark blue uniforms and carrying swords. Nobody wanted to retreat, but with twenty thousand casualties in two days of combat, nobody was suggesting an attack. Finally, it was settled that the Army of the Potomac would stay put and wait and see what Robert E. Lee would decide to do.

"If he does attack tomorrow," Meade said, as the men filed out into the moonlight, "it will be in the middle. He's tried both flanks and failed. Tomorrow he'll hit the center."

"Cus . . . *Custis*. . . ."

There was motion, then a cough.

"Shhhhhhh — " Wes whispered, "don't make a sound. Custis, *listen.*"

It was not quite light, but there was a tingling brightness in the air, a wave of freshness blowing over their heads. Birds were waking in the branches. Custis untangled himself from sleep, eyes gritty, a foot gone numb. "What's going on?"

"I hear somebody . . . maybe a whole lot of somebodies. . . ."

Wes swung his gun up over the side of the trench. Both men were alert, straining to hear. Behind a thick screen of fog twigs snapped and the sound of heavy footsteps scraped against the hill.

"See anything?"

"Not yet."

"Dumb me," said Custis. "How could I expect you to see anything. This trench is taller than you are!"

"Now quit fooling," Wes hissed. "We've got to get out of here."

"Yep, it's moving day, all right. Let's go!"

They eased out of the trench, and glided up the slope to take shelter in the underbrush. Morning exploded in a burst of shellfire. Tree limbs crashed heavily to earth. They heard distant shouts, the brittle snap of musketry. A figure charged past them and vanished behind the thick trunk of an oak.

"What's going on?" Custis called out softly.

The brim of a slouch hat poked out. "The bluebellies came back and found us in their hidey-holes. Come on, we're going up!"

"Again?" Custis sighed. "I sure hope your Uncle

Henry's got the coffee boiling." There were furious shouts from below, and thick rapid thumps of artillery. A horse clattered up over the rocks, and plunged in among the trees; the major, trim and upright, called to them, gesturing with his sword. Minie balls flew in among the branches, ripping white scars open on the trunks of trees.

Custis glanced at Wes and said quietly, "I'll see you at the top, friend." The major was out in the open again, the haunches of his horse moving powerfully, like dark, shining water. Custis had never felt so alive. He felt the blood pulsing through him, the hard muscular leap of his heart. Gun ready, his eyes picked out every shadow of movement. This time they would do it, he was certain. *That crazy joy.* Ahead, the major's raised sword arced across the brightening light.

A line of Union sharpshooters stepped out from under the trees. Custis heard his own sharp cough of surprise, felt his bare feet splay out from under him, thought *Bekah,* and was gone.

18

SHE WAS STARTLED AWAKE.

"I'm sorry." The man's voice was quiet, very low in the dim room. Pale light glowed at the window. "I was dreaming and I must have called out. Did I wake you?"

"It wasn't you." Bekah stood up, her hair hanging loose and damp and tangled down her back, her heart still thumping with fright. There were more deep, rumbling explosions from the southeast. "It was the guns." She went to the bedside. "Do you need something for the pain?"

"Not yet. It makes me drowsy, and I want to be awake. Have you had any news?"

"Some rebels came in the night, but they didn't tell us anything about the battle. They brought two wounded men . . . they had to find a place for them." Her hands were busy, raising the captain against the feather pillows, smoothing the covers. There was a tremor in her voice. "One man wouldn't stop bleeding. We tried to help him, but he died. The other one is badly hurt, too. Mother's with him now." She wrung out a cloth in a basin of water and carefully bathed the captain's face.

"You look very tired," he said.

She had slept a little in her clothes in the chair by

the window. For the first time she noticed the stiff dark stains all over her dress. "If only we had been able to stop the bleeding. . . ."

"I'm sure you did all that you could."

"Leander wanted to go out and find a doctor, but we couldn't let him leave the house in the dark; it was just too dangerous. Besides, nobody would have had the time to come . . . there are too many others." There were two deep explosions, one heavy sound piled on top of another. "I'm worried. Those guns are firing close to here, and I have a cousin somewhere around Culp's Hill."

"A Union man?"

"No, he's with the Confederate army. But he's a fine person, Captain. You'd like him, really you would."

"That's what's so strange and tragic about all of this," he said. "Friends fighting friends, kin against kin. . . . It's all so wrong and unnatural. Here we are, two armies desperate to win, and all the time there's this queer . . . *respect* . . . between us."

"My brother Buck could be here . . . fighting Custis and his brother Mason . . . and they love each other!"

He said gently, "You have a lot on your mind, Bekah. I've been a trouble to you."

"Please . . . ," she put a hand on his shoulder, "I'm glad that you've been here for me to care for. It takes my mind off all the rest. Now I'm going to make you some tea."

Leander, sleepy and rumpled and unwashed, brought up the tray.

"You've had a hard night, Leander?"

"Yes, sir. A man died downstairs. And the other one won't let my mother leave him, not for a minute. He keeps talking about his wife and children, asking her to look at their pictures. He made her promise to let his family know when. . . ." The boy took a deep shaky breath. "When I used to think about the war, I never thought about *that*."

"The dying? No, I don't suppose that you did. And that's what war is all about, Leander . . . an accumulation of *little* deaths that piles up into enormous grief." The captain let himself be helped to sip the tea, and then he leaned back against the pillows, his face twisting with pain as he tried to find a comfortable position.

"Captain Waite?" Leander pulled up a chair and sat down. "Why did you choose the cavalry?"

"My father was a blacksmith. I grew up around horses, and I've loved them all my life. It seemed the natural thing to do." He smiled. "Not that I hadn't heard the old joke."

"What joke?"

"That nobody has ever seen a dead cavalryman. I guess it's true that we were pretty useless at the start. The Southern men were better riders, more experienced with the animals. We had a lot to learn. But we did catch on. The army has learned a great deal, Leander. We have good guns and ammunition, and plenty of food and supplies. The Confederacy is slowly starving. It's getting harder and harder for the South to feed its men, equip them, replace them. In the end we may not break them at all, because their spirit is incredible . . . but we may just wear them out. That's what General Grant is doing now at Vicksburg."

Bekah came back into the room and stood at the window looking off in the direction of the gunfire. She had changed her dress and tidied her hair. Outside the noise was growing louder, more intense. "When will it stop? I wish it would stop!" She glanced over her shoulder at the captain. "What if we did let the South go? Then all of this would be over. Father said we had to preserve the Union, but maybe it isn't that important." She stared off toward Culp's Hill. "I shouldn't have said that. I know it's a terrible thing to say."

"More and more are saying the very same thing," the captain told her, "the longer the war goes on. Many people are wondering if it's worth the effort."

"Do you think it is?" Leander asked.

"Yes, but what I think isn't that important. Our President believes it is, and he has a longer, clearer vision than the rest of us. He knows that if the country divides, then this unique experiment of ours . . . this democracy . . . will have failed. He doesn't want that to happen. But unless it works for all of us, then it has no true meaning: our system would have been built on a lie that says we are all created equal."

"My cousins think that people in the South treat colored folk just fine," Leander said. "He says we don't understand how it really is."

"But it's a bigger issue than how one man treats his

slaves, isn't it? What about his right even to own another human being? If the North wins then that will be settled for once and for all."

Bekah said, "I think I understand the reasons for the war. It's just hard to make sense of so many dying . . . like the man downstairs, and the ones lying in the street and out in the fields. There was a song we used to sing at the beginning when we sent away the soldiers. 'O! It is Sweet for Our Country to Die!' I thought it was so beautiful, so true."

She remembered the song, the passionate partings. Prayers, and preachers with raised arms almost flying from the pulpit in praise of all the volunteers. Ceremonies and patriotic speeches and men in blue uniforms huddled under bright swags of bunting, proud of the public fuss. Banquets and bouquets. She remembered the cheers, the clapping hands, and the high-hearted, off-key bands, and flag after flag after flag, endlessly streaming. She had stood in a white dress, with flowers at her breast, knowing that her strong voice filled the auditorium as she sang.

> O! It is sweet for our country to die,
> How softly reposes
> Warrior youth on his bier,
> Wet by the tears of his love. . . .

How easy it had been to imagine God nodding and approving, majestically in tune with the cause of the Union.

> O! Then how great for our country to die,
> In the front rank to perish. . . .

140

"There's nothing sweet or great about dead soldiers," she said. "Now that I've seen them, I know."

All morning the fight for Culp's Hill pounded on
in the summer heat. Slocum's men, returning at
dawn, surprised and were surprised by enemy soldiers
in the trenches they had abandoned when they had
gone out to help the Third Corps, and the struggle to
possess the high ground went on for hours. Support
finally arrived for the thin Union defense crouched
behind log breastworks at the top of the hill, and
slowly the Southern troops were worried back, beaten
farther down the rough, splintered slopes. By late
morning the noise of the artillery had stopped, with
only an occasional minie ball hissing in among the
trees, scattering leaves, chewing through bark.

At noon, quiet. A violent storm had blown across
the hillside, ripped through the pleasant woods,
blasted rows of bodies down against the ground. Near
the summit a small, dark-bearded man sprawled face
down, lying close to a light-haired, smooth-faced boy
spread-eagled on his back. An eerie hush passed over
them like wind, swept through the shattered trees,
spread out along the heated ridges. In a burning
midday silence tens of thousands of soldiers waited,
listening for some sound that would break the tension
and signal the beginning of the end.

A peculiar calm on the field. Continued chaos in
the streets of Gettysburg as carts and wagons brought
in the endless loads of wounded men.

* * *

"You shouldn't go out there now," Bekah told her mother. "There are too many sharpshooters."

"I have to go." Mrs. Summerhill had forgotten to take her nerve medicine and was ignoring a headache that pulsed angrily over one eye. Many of the townspeople were going to the college and the schools, churches, and warehouses to help feed and bathe the thousands of casualties. In their houses men, women, and children were picking lint, rolling bandages, cooking food, caring for the men who had been brought to their doors.

"Then I'll go with you," Bekah said.

"No, I want you to stay here. There's still the Captain to look after, and it doesn't seem right to leave those other poor men alone."

"Mother . . . they're dead."

"I know. But if they were in their own homes someone would be sitting by and mourning them. Leander and I will slip down to the church and see what we can do. Take care, Bekah."

"You be careful, too."

Bekah hurried past the closed parlor door, ashamed of her feeling of dread at being left alone with the bodies. She thought of the soldiers' families waiting to hear news of the battle. She would have to write and tell them what had happened.

Beef broth simmered on the kitchen stove, and as she stirred it she heard a knocking at the front of the house.

It was a young Confederate soldier supporting an older man with gray, untidy whiskers and dazed, mournful eyes. A bloody rag was twisted around his head.

"Bring him in," Bekah said. "Is he badly hurt?"

"He got knocked on the side of the head, and part of his ear is tore off, but I think he'll be all right if he can lie down somewhere." He nodded at the closed parlor door. "Do you want me to put him in there?"

She thought quickly. Not there, and not upstairs where he might discover Adam Waite. "In the kitchen." There was a faded sofa where her father had liked to take a nap every day after dinner. She helped ease the older man down, and then she propped pillows behind his back. He sighed and closed his eyes.

"Was he hurt in that fight this morning?"

"Yes, miss. Culp's Hill they call it. . . . You must know where that is."

"Yes, I know. We go there often for picnics."

"There was no picnic there today. Your boys finally took hold of it, but a lot of poor fellers got killed." He looked at the pot of broth steaming on the stove, and Bekah saw the hunger in his eyes.

"It's almost ready. Would you like some?"

"Please, miss. And my friend here. It would perk him up some."

She cut the last slices from a loaf and ladled the soup into bowls. The soldier swallowed his greedily with great, noisy gulps as Bekah sat beside the man on the sofa and helped him take some nourishment from a spoon. He was too tired and weak, and soon he lay back and closed his eyes again. She pitied him.

He was much too old to fight. Something would have to be done about his injury. She put the kettle on the stove to warm some water.

"Is the battle over yet?" she asked.

"Oh, no, miss!" The young soldier folded a piece of bread and crammed it into his mouth. As he chewed he looked at her with bright confident eyes. "Our guns are lined up as far as you can see along that ridge across the valley. Marse Robert ain't about to quit. By tonight your fellers will be scattered halfway to Baltimore."

She said nothing more while he finished eating. When he was gone, she bathed the old man's head wound and put on a fresh bandage. Exhausted, he went back to sleep, and she decided to take some hot broth upstairs to the captain. She had just reached for a bowl when she heard a noise in the hall. Leander was standing there staring at her. Then he came slowly into the kitchen, his skin so pale it looked almost blue, like the color of skim milk. All his freckles stood out in sharp, dark points. "Leander? What is it?"

His face worked as he tried to hold back tears.

Bekah grabbed his arms. "Tell me. What's happened?"

"Jennie."

"Jennie Wade? What about her?"

His lips moved stiffly. "Shot. In the back. She was baking, and a minie ball came through two doors and killed her."

Bekah let go of him. Neither of them said anything. Then Leander left the kitchen, and the front door opened and softly closed. Moments later Bekah realized that she should have stopped him, that what had happened to Jennie Wade could easily happen to someone else. She didn't want to believe what he had told her. Instead she tried to remember the chores that she should do, but it was as if a door had slammed shut in her mind. For a long time she sat, hands clamped together on the kitchen table, unable to move or think. Finally she got up and took a bowl of broth up to Adam Waite.

"Bekah, do you know what time it is?"

"It's almost one o'clock."

He seemed puzzled by the silence. "It's very quiet, isn't it?"

"Yes."

"Is there any news?"

"I just talked with a rebel who brought in another wounded man a while ago. The battle isn't over yet, but he says by tonight our army will be scattered halfway to Baltimore."

"It's going badly for us, then?" he said when he had finished eating. With a sigh he leaned back against the pillows.

"Nobody knows. The rebels still have the town, but our men took Culp's Hill this morning. A lot of soldiers were killed."

She put the bowl and spoon on the tray, her face turned away from him.

"You're thinking of your cousin, aren't you?"

She picked up the tray and started toward the door.

"Wait — don't go away!"

"There's a sick man downstairs. . . ."

"Please come here." He looked up into her face. "You've been crying, haven't you? Bekah, your cousin is probably safe and well. You'll have word from him soon."

"It isn't just Custis . . . a friend was killed this morning by a sharpshooter. She was only a few doors away. We loved Jennie Wade. . . . She was going to be married soon."

He reached out, touched her arm. "I'm so sorry. You people shouldn't be involved. A young lady like you should never have to see such terrible things."

"But now I know." She sat on the side of the bed. "Now everyone in Gettysburg knows what this thing is really like. I don't think I'm a stupid girl, Captain . . . but when I think of how thrilled and excited my friends and I were when we sent the men away, and how the bands played and we sang and listened to the speeches and *applauded*. . . . I feel ashamed at how naive I was. I swear we enjoyed it. After all, we weren't a part of it. Maybe if more of us had known what it meant, we would have tried to do something to stop it."

Downstairs the clock struck, its golden chime rising through the stillness of the house.

"And Buck . . . I swear he was in love with it, too. I wonder how he feels about it now."

19

FIRST THERE WAS PAIN, THEN THIRST. IT WAS HARD to decide which tortured him the most. Memory limped back slowly. Buck remembered the screaming place, moths banging in against the smoking lanterns, a jagged and peculiar sound. His leg hurt badly. He was relieved to know that they had saved it, and yet he was afraid to look, to know for sure. When he did, stiffly raising his neck to see, he discovered that there was nothing left below one knee. He cried.

Later he called for water, pleading for it over and over, louder and louder, but when nobody came he stopped asking, knowing that if he spent himself uselessly that way he would soon die.

He lay in a field with hundreds, possibly thousands of others, and yet he felt completely alone in his misery. The sun was high in the sky, its fierce white light burning his face, almost blinding him. He thought of the house on Baltimore Street, the tall clock quietly ticking in the hallway, the dark carved bedstead in his room, with its soft feather mattress and smooth, cool linen. It was the one place on earth he wanted to be.

* * *

Both ends had been tested, and there was only the middle left to try. Wright's brigade had punched through there yesterday, and if he had had support, today might have been a different story. Yet what had been done by a few could certainly be done again, this time by thousands of fresh, willing troops.

"Would you eat something, sir?"

"Not now. Maybe later. But nothing special, Taylor. Whatever is in the pot."

Both of them recognized the change, the upswing. Everything was ready this time, a hundred and fifty guns already in place with bright young Alexander in charge of the artillery today. Longstreet was still sullen, but he would give the signal when the cannonade had softened up the center of the Union line. Then close to fifteen thousand soldiers, with General Pickett in charge, would advance across the valley and overwhelm *those people*.

Lee smiled thinking of George Pickett. Scented, exuberant, with long childish curls. Charming, always charming. A grown man still boyishly in love with glory. And Sallie with the sunset eyes, a girl just half his age, how he enjoyed dashing letters off to her in moments of high passion, sometimes in the noise of battle! He was probably writing to her now.

God must decide it. One last long slope to climb, and then the Army of Northern Virginia would carry victory back home to the South. Grace and civility and tradition. This northern land was a foreign place, a separate country after all. There was a hardness here, a flinty people; he had thought so at West

148

Point. How could such different cultures ever blend in peace?

"Sir? What do you think?"

The lieutenant looked across the valley at the row of guns that bristled from the Seminary building down to a point opposite the peach orchard. "I'd say they have about twice as many as we do, but," Alonzo Cushing, an extraordinarily handsome officer, smiled, "I think we're twice as good."

"What's going to happen?"

"They'll probably hammer at us for a while, and then they'll send their infantry over."

"All that way? It must be a mile."

"I don't believe they'll make it, not if we give them everything we've got."

"Then how come they believe it?"

"Confidence, I guess. They've always had it, and it's usually worked. Not this time, though. Not here."

"Strange, isn't it?" Sergeant Fuger sank down beside the cannon, and rested his back against the wheel. "It's so quiet I can hear the bees."

Lieutenant Cushing heard them, too, a soothing blur winding among the familiar clink and jingle of harness and the stamp of horses' hooves, the faint orders shouted farther down the line, the laughter and conversation. Battery A, U.S. Artillery, was parked near an angle of a low stone wall, close to the only clump of trees to be seen along the length of Cemetery Ridge. Some of Cushing's crew sat relaxing in the little grove of oak and chestnut, and some lay stretched out on their backs staring drowsily up into the cloudless sky. Ahead, behind the wall, the Second Corps men rested, hot sunshine beating down upon their heads.

A shudder. Another shudder. Then *crash, crash, crash, crash* bounded across the valley in a crushing avalanche of sound, the hazy air vibrating as the long-range missiles streaked overhead and struck and struck and struck. Union officers, picnicking on the sunny backside of the ridge, scattered as the first shells exploded; within minutes Federal guns were returning fire; artillerymen were ramming, firing, sponging, reloading. Shells roared past in both directions, the shock of the cannonade like a gigantic wind, sending rolling waves across the wheatfield.

Soon the noise was so intense that Alonzo Cushing couldn't hear his own guns firing. There was plenty of damage being done to the batteries along the line, and yet he saw that many of the enemy explosives were landing on the reverse of the slope where the reserve ammunition and supply wagons were parked. It was supposed to be the safest place on the battlefield, and yet it was here that stunned noncombatants, sutlers and musicians, wagon drivers and stragglers, even the wounded lying helpless on the ground, were caught in a wild flurry of screeching, whistling, moaning chunks of whirling metal. He thought, *They can't see our infantry, they think it's back there, that's why they're aiming too high.*

He had never before, in any battle, heard such a collision of sound. Crews worked mechanically, obediently, all parts of one devastating machine. For three days the battle had been building pressure, and now it was hissing hot, boiling over, a whistling kettle of fury.

In the Leister farmhouse, a few hundred yards to the rear, George Meade agreed reluctantly to move. The roar outside was impossible, and bit by bit the place was being ripped away. The front steps were already gone; one pillar and then another had been knocked off the porch. A shell skipped through the yard, slid to a stop, and lay there intact.

As they left the house the general and his staff were appalled to see so many of their horses, tethered to a nearby fence, dead and grotesquely dangling. A growling object spun through the door jamb, and exploded inside the building they had just left.

"All right!" Meade muttered. "We're going!"

"Where, sir?" His aide winced as another missile screeched through a lilac bush, spraying them with leaves and clumps of dirt.

"Slocum's headquarters at Power's Hill."

"Sir?"

"Slocum's headquarters!"

"Very good, sir. You'll be quite safe there."

Meade fixed him with angry, bulging eyes. "I don't care about safe — I just want my orders to be heard!"

"Sir?"

"Go! For God's sake, go!"

"Scared?"

Huddled behind the stone wall, Charlie Payne

poked his friend. George Dawson cupped an ear to show he couldn't hear.

"I ASKED IF YOU WAS SCARED!"

This time George understood and grinned and shook his curly head. Private Payne felt better. George was so big and solid and steady; as long as he stuck close to him he felt protected. And it did seem as if the worst of it was flying over them. He glanced over his shoulder, saw in one brilliant flash a caisson explode, wheels, limbs of horses and men, and pieces of timber scattering through the air.

He reached into his pocket for his watch. He wasn't quite sure when the uproar had first started, but it was now almost two o'clock. He had never heard the likes of this. It was, he figured, the loudest racket of the war, of any war, the most monumental racket ever heard upon the continent.

Now he was poked.

George had tucked both hands beneath his chin, dropped his eyelashes, and was playfully pretending to be asleep.

Charlie laughed. There was something stupefying about a roar that heavy and monotonous. Sweat dripped steadily down his face, and he guessed he knew how it felt to be roasted alive. Squinting up, he saw the sun, a scorched red spot burning through a thick blanket of soiled smoke. He glanced at the soldier squatting beside him. George was slumped forward, his head on his knees, no longer pretending, but sound asleep.

* * *

Colonel E. P. Alexander, in charge of Confederate artillery on this sweltering afternoon, had been tossed a problem so hot that, as he juggled it mentally, he looked for some way to get rid of it. He resented the message that had just arrived from General Longstreet. If the massive bombardment didn't do the job and drive off or greatly demoralize the enemy, Old Pete had written, then he, Alexander, was to advise General Pickett not to make the charge! That was it. In a few words Longstreet had left it up to him, a subordinate, to decide at the most critical moment of the three-day battle whether or not fifteen thousand soldiers should cross the valley and attack the entrenched Army of the Potomac.

"How am I supposed to know what's going on over there?" Alexander peered through the murky cloud that now shrouded the opposite ridge. His eyes were raw with strain. Union fire was still intense, uninterrupted. "I can't even *see* their infantry. God knows they ought to be demoralized, but how can I tell for sure?" Exasperated, he handed the message over to General Wright. "What do you make of this?"

The other officer scanned the paper, and shrugged. "I think General Longstreet is looking for a way out. He doesn't want to send anyone over there, but he's had his orders."

"Then he'll have to find his own way out." Alexander scribbled a reply. The only way he could tell what effect the bombardment was having on the enemy was by the return fire, he wrote, as he couldn't see the infantry. Therefore, if there was an alternative to the proposed attack, it ought to be carefully considered. Ammunition was running low, and if Pickett's charge didn't succeed, there would be none left to support another. He sent the message back to Longstreet.

Now. Back to business.

Henry Hunt, chief of the Union artillery, was having problems of his own. Down a long, roaring tunnel of time, hundreds of missiles had been sent across the smoking valley, but the bombardment couldn't go on forever. Eventually the rebels were going to charge, and when they did he must make certain that nobody made it up the grassy slope to break through the iron corridor that stretched from Cemetery Hill out to the Round Tops.

Better to have his men reserve their fire now, and save their ammunition until the actual assault.

He was annoyed, then, when his order to do this was squelched by General Hancock. The Superb he was called and he acted the part. On this booming day, among dust and fumes and dangerous spinning fragments, he was, as always, a marvel and a mystery. Hunt could never understand how the big man could come from the rubble of battle with snowy cuffs and a dazzling shirtfront, looking as coolly impeccable as if he had just attended a formal banquet. Yesterday he had been everywhere, planting batteries and sending in reinforcements to plug the broken line as he tried to patch up Sickles's blunder. Today, in the middle of the cannonade, he had continued to plunge up and down the ridge on horseback.

Now Hancock was insisting that the bombardment must go on. "If our men think that the artillery is weakening, softening up, then they'll lose heart."

Obediently the deafened gunners continued to load missiles into the long, heated barrels of the guns.

Across the valley Colonel Alexander received another message from Longstreet.

> The intention is to advance the infantry if the artillery has the desired effect of driving the enemy off, or having other effect such as to warrant us in making the attack. When the moment arrives advise General Pickett and of course advance such artillery as you can use in aiding the attack.

The same sizzling bomb, right back in his lap again. Longstreet seemed determined to leave it up to him. Alexander went to look for Pickett, and found the general cheerfully writing a letter. He seemed confident and eager to make the attack. Encouraged, Alexander sent a reply to his superior.

> When our artillery fire is at its best I will advise General Pickett to advance.

A mile away Hunt had finally had his way. One by one the big Federal guns were shutting down, cooling off as the crews dragged away the damaged batteries, eighteen from Cemetery Hill. All along the blasted line men rushed in to carry away the dead and injured.

"What's going on?" George Dawson opened his eyes, snatched off his cap, and rubbed his damp hair.

Charlie laughed. "Nothing. It's the silence . . . that's what woke you up."

"You mean it's all over?"

Charlie felt uneasy in the sudden lull. "I've got a notion . . . that it's just about to start."

George Pickett, his long curls bouncing out from under his perky hat, rode up to General Longstreet and saluted. For a few moments the older officer stared back, and when he finally spoke his voice was so hoarse and low that it was difficult for the younger man to understand him.

"I'm being crucified at the thought of the sacrifice of life which this attack will make. . . ." Longstreet glanced away, struggling for control. The sad eyes lifted. "I've instructed Alexander to watch the effect of our fire upon the enemy, and when it begins to tell. . . ." Once more his voice broke off as he sat, heavy, troubled, unwilling to say what he had to say to this exuberant man he was fond of. "Then he must take the responsibility and give you your orders, for I can't."

A messenger arrived, slipped down from his horse, and quickly approached Pickett with a note. When he had read it the general handed it to Longstreet.

For God's sake come quick. The eighteen guns are
gone; come quick, or my ammunition won't let me
support you properly.

"Should I obey this?"

Longstreet held out his hand, put his other one on
Pickett's, and silently bowed his head.

"Then, General . . . I'll lead my division in now."

As Pickett got on his horse he remembered the letter he had written to Sallie. On the corner of the envelope he had scribbled *If Old Peter's nod means death,
then goodbye and God bless you, little one.* He took it out of
his pocket. "Sir? Would you be good enough to mail
this for me?"

Longstreet took it and turned away. Pickett was
startled to see that his cheeks and his beard were wet.

"I don't want to make this charge," Longstreet said
to Alexander a short time later. "I don't see how it
can succeed. I wouldn't make it now, but General Lee
has ordered it, and is expecting it."

20

SLOWLY THE BITTER SMOKE DRIFTED UP AND AWAY.
The sun emerged, a cheerful blaze of yellow from behind the haze. Off in the tall grass Mason Walker
heard a soldier recite:

> "Backward, roll backward,
> O Time in thy flight.
> Make me a child again,
> Just for this fight.

And a mocking voice replied, "Yes, and a gal child at
that!"

There was laughter and joking among the men,
and then an abrupt shouted, "Attention!"

A tingling hush spread among the troops. Mason
felt the familiar trembling in his limbs, the knot
tightening in his belly, the dryness in his mouth. Soldiers gulped water from canteens, nodded to friends,
put away letters and testaments. Some prayed, eyes
closed, lips moving. Most stood passively waiting.
The final order came from a buoyant Pickett:

"Column forward! Guide center!"

Men pushed forward, thousands of them, soft-col-
ored in faded uniforms and ragged homespun, moving out of the woods and across the top of the ridge,
passing the long glint of the silent guns, heading

down the slope. A band played somewhere, a bright tune strutting off across the valley. Mason heard voices call faintly, "Goodbye, boys . . . goodbye . . ." and caught, from the corner of his eye, a tall, gray, watchful presence on the crest.

No cheers, no sense of hurry, only the solid rustling motion of a mile of men, pouring across the swales in the direction of a spray of trees sketched delicately upon the distant ridge. Pickett's brigades to the right, Garnett's to the left, Armistead's men at the rear. And, since Heth wasn't well today, Pettigrew and Trimble would guide his troops in at the far left. March step. Battle flags brilliantly fluttering.

"Some of the fellows were talking," said the man next to Mason, "about General Armistead. Seems he went to West Point with General Hancock . . . they were best friends there. And now Hancock's waiting over there for us . . . for him. Queer, isn't it?"

"Yes," Mason said, his breath going out of him in quick ragged pants. "It's queer, all right." A warning buzz crackled through his brain, and over the familiar terror new shocks of fear flashed through him. Strange, too strange, this measured walk across an open plain straight into the muzzles of those waiting cannons.

Lee was no fool. He never wasted men, he must believe it could be done. Pickett, too, was preened for it, and yet all of Mason's instincts screamed at him to turn around, to run the other way. *Can't! File-closers would stop me, too disgraceful!* His body trembled, muscles shaking with the effort to keep moving forward, knees almost giving way as he concentrated on pushing first one forward, then the other.

"Keep up, son . . ." murmured the veteran next to him. He was calm-faced, in control, as casual as Custis. "Keep up. . . ."

"Tell you what," Mason swallowed, gave the man a wry, lopsided grin, "if you get there first, you save a place for me."

"Look! My God, here they come!"

Amazement, lightning swift, electrified the Union soldiers waiting by the guns, crouching behind scraped piles of dirt and stones, hiding behind earth-and-rail breastworks. "Here comes their infantry!"

"George!" Charlie Payne peered across the protective wall. "George, take a look at that! Have you ever seen anything like it?"

His friend stared in silence, his big jaw dropped in wonder.

No one expected beauty on a battlefield. Yet here it was, the cruel splendor of thousands of soldiers parading across the summer fields in a shimmering spectacle of sunbright steel and polished bayonets and swaying silken flags. Lovely, and terrible as any nightmare, with no chance of waking. Then the ugly thunder of the cannons broke again; missiles burst from the Union guns, exploding in the long, low cloud of marching men, the glamorous shapes grayghostly now behind thick piles of rising smoke.

"They're coming straight at us!" George Dawson cried. His excited voice was almost a shriek. "We've got to stop them!"

Charlie glanced at him, surprised. "We will." He gripped his rifle with slippery fingers. "Soon as we get them in our range, we will."

George knelt, wildly firing. *"Stop them! Stop them! Stop them!"*

Charlie grabbed his arm. "Quit wasting cartridges, you fool. They'll be here soon enough."

He couldn't believe that George was acting in such a crazy way.

There was nothing to do but wait. Batteries on Cemetery Hill, along the ridge, and near the Round Tops were sending hundreds of shells screaming into the advance. Charlie could see parts of it dissolving, men disappearing, others pushing up from behind to fill in the holes as the gray mass rolled closer, still coming on steadily, getting nearer.

Lieutenant Cushing had pushed Battery A up to the angle at the stone wall, just ahead of the small clump of trees that had shaded some of his crew as they ate their noon meal. From his new position he had the eerie sensation that the whole rebel army was headed directly at him, was funneling in toward the muzzles of his guns. He was ready. Heavy metal cans were in place beside each piece, and at three hundred and fifty yards he would order the single charge, at a hundred yards the double and the triple. He was confident no one would get closer than that.

Far to the left, Vermonters, angled out into the valley, watched nervously as the first line of enemy soldiers approached within their rifle range.

"Make ready. . . . Aim low. . . . On your feet. . . . Fire!"

There was a sharp crackle. Dozens of men went down, their comrades ignoring them, ignoring the Vermonters, pressing steadily ahead. Elation rippled through the New England regiment. This was the first battle they had experienced, and the thing they had most feared seemed almost simple now. Firing, reloading, firing again, they cut down soldiers who refused to look at them or notice them, who fell or passed on by with eyes fixed stubbornly upon some distant point.

"Whoo — ee!" A young recruit dug for a cartridge, eager to get off another shot. He aimed and fired, and a man in butternut crashed forward through the smoke. "Whoo — eee!" the Vermonter screamed again. "It's like shooting ducks on the lake back home!"

His regiment wheeled and caught the advance on the oblique, slaughtering dozens more as the movement flowed past.

On the right, the 8th Ohio, placed dangerously forward on the valley floor, watched the great, proud, gleaming lines push closer to the Emmitsburg Road, colors flickering, a mounted officer gesturing in the direction of a clump of trees. Closer to them a North Carolinian brigade was seen to hesitate as shells blew ragged holes across their ranks. Then suddenly, in the swaying confusion, men were turning, running, fading off across the smoke-blurred field. Coolly, accurately, the Ohioans continued to pump cartridges into the exposed left flank of the Virginians still sweeping on toward the grassy slope ahead.

"Hear that?" one man shouted to another.

"I hear it. Makes my skin crawl."

It was a curious hum rising from men advancing with their heads bent low, leaning into the storm of killing hail. Ahead of them muskets waited, and mutilating sprays of metal balls that could spatter them to pieces, but still they came on, frustration whining in their throats, surrounding them with a mournful roar.

General Armistead had placed his hat on the tip of his sword, and it was the bold flight of the black hat flapping forward across the valley that had guided what was left of his brigade.

Now and then Mason glimpsed the landmark trees, then lost them again in bursts of spreading smoke. His legs moved faster; he heard the sharp rasp of breath scratching harshly in his throat. The man who had said, "Keep up, son," was gone, the one who had replaced him blown away, and hundreds, maybe thousands left scattered far behind, yet the terrible quaking that had shaken the boy from the beginning had disappeared. He felt he was part of a lethal marching machine that could not be stopped, that he was one of Pickett's men, the bravest and the best, and there was no fear in him, only the will to lift the machine higher, to drive it through the bright rim of fire just ahead. The vast, sparkling mass of the division was reduced now to a jostling mob that rushed up an incline toward an angle in a low stone wall. Mason heard minie balls hissing through the thick, sour air and noisy cheers as cannisters discharged at pointblank range. He stumbled across a headless form splashed on the slope, twisted to his feet, moved on as colors lifted up the rise. Then he was cresting the ridge on the shrill scream of the Virginians as a black hat soared high and flew away out of sight.

Charlie Payne watched them coming, bitter with knowing that his best friend had run, as others around him were running. Behind him an officer screamed, "Halt! Halt, you cowards! Face about! Fire!"

"The hell, then," Charlie wept. "The hell with you, George." He crouched, eyes wet with anger, as a black hat held high on a sword sailed toward him through the air.

At Battery A, Alonzo Cushing gasped orders as he tried to close the terrible gash at his groin with both hands. "I'll give them one last shot. . . ." A bullet crashed through the roof of his mouth, and he slumped into Sergeant Fuger's arms.

Charlie Payne sprang to his feet and grabbed for the soldier leaping in through a gap in the wall. He took him by the throat and shook and shook, his fingers squeezing, as he growled *"You — you — you. . . ."* But he couldn't speak the name of what it was he wanted to destroy, as more of the enemy poured through, became a mob that seethed around him,

164

lashing back from the angle into the little grove of trees beyond. Men in blue were running forward, piling in from the far side of the ridge, crowding up from all directions, pistols and revolvers firing, eager to kick in the end of the battle, to smash it, finish it. Lewis Armistead, with a hand on one of the Union cannons, went down, the hat knocked from his sword and trampled in the dirt.

Mason struggled, fighting for breath, pinwheels of light exploding in his brain. The hands at his throat relaxed; with a low grunt the body that was gripping him slid away, taking him down as a slouch-hatted man wearing butternut raised a wet bayonet, and whirled away with a triumphant yell. Mason curled in against the wall, gasping to suck in air, hearing the battle roar roll away from him. Slowly he pulled himself up and crawled to his knees, meeting the shocked pale stare of Private Payne.

"It was a bayonet...." He felt an urgent need to explain what had happened. "We were fighting man to man . . . that's how it was. . . . And you were stronger, but somebody...." He stopped, feeling foolish. There was nothing more to say. The soldier's eyes were clean of rage and peacefully staring.

Mason got to his feet. Prisoners were being rounded up, hustled off to the rear; officers hoarsely shouted orders up and down the line and guns still popped and cracked along the ridge, but the frenzy had gone from the fight and Mason knew it was over, knew they had failed. Already ambulance crews were hurrying in among the wailing casualties. Glancing down the slope he saw pale dabs of running men blending into the smoke that clung across the valley. High in the sky the sun was powdered over with a dirty haze.

"Keep still, boy — don't mess with me." Mason was yanked from behind, his arms firmly held. He did not resist. In his year of war he had never felt as drained or as hopeless as he did now. There was a drabness in him, a dead, gray, heavy weariness.

Near him, on the ground, General Armistead spoke softly to a Union officer who bent over him, listening.

"He wants to speak to General Hancock," the man called to another. "Does anyone know where he is?"

Someone answered, "He's been badly hurt . . . he's been taken off the field."

Mason saw that Armistead would die, as thousands of others had died in this terrible miscalculation. A mile of valiant soldiers wasted. Something fierce and proud and irreplaceable had been broken on this hard Pennsylvania ridge. He ached for Lee. Surely it would break the great man's heart.

But the fear, at last, was gone.

He was shoved into a thick blue roar of cheering men. His captor moved him slowly toward the rear, not jerking or bullying him, but looking at him with curious eyes. He was a solid, amiable man, with rough yellow curls hanging below his cap. "You're sure a little fry. How old are you, son?"

"Seventeen."

"Tuckered out, ain't you?"

Mason nodded.

"I never seen the likes of it," George Dawson said. "You fellers kind of took our breath away. But we whipped you. Reckon it was time."

Mason said nothing.

"Don't suppose you'd have a chaw on you. I sure do like that good tobacco."

The boy shook his head. He wished he had some to give to the friendly man, but he didn't use tobacco.

The private held up a canteen, jiggled it slyly. "Want some commissary, son? Might help you feel better."

"No, thank you."

Mason had promised his mother that he wouldn't touch hard liquor until he was twenty-one. There were still four years to go before he was of age.

21

"THEY'RE GOING TO LEAVE US HERE, AIN'T THEY?" asked a soldier, shot through both thighs, who was lying close to Buck in the rough, scorched field. "Leave us here to rot. They'll plant potatoes in us come next spring."

"Listen," Buck whispered. "Listen. . . ."

A roar thickened in the distance, cheer after cheer,

full-throated, jubilant. "Maybe it's over . . . maybe we've won. . . ."

The wounded man next to him paid no attention to the sound. Nothing mattered to him but his private battle with his own fear and pain. For hours he had moaned, sobbed, and hiccoughed like a child. "Ain't just the thirst that's killing me," he whined. "It's the flies — crawlin' in my eyes and mouth. . . ."

"Flies won't kill you." Yet Buck also had a horror of the blue-black insects that sizzled and crawled over every part of his body. In spells of terror during the night he had been sure he felt them breeding in his brain.

"First they shot me, then them rebel bastards robbed me, then they left me," the man said. "And now I'm dumped out here like trash. At least somebody done somethin' for you. You're the lucky one . . . it ain't fair. . . ."

The lucky one. That seemed funny to Buck, and his chest began to heave up and down in silent laughter. After a while he stopped laughing because it tired him. "You're alive," he said. His voice was cracked and dried out, like old leather. "So stay alive." He said it more for himself than for the other man. He couldn't hold out much longer without water. Earlier, men had swayed through the field with brimming buckets, and run out just before they reached him. "You'll come back?" he'd pleaded when they left, and they had promised to return, but that was . . . hours ago? Yesterday, maybe. He did not believe they would ever come back.

"Don't let me die," whimpered the soldier.

"It's not up to me." Buck was angry in his helplessness. "It's up to you. Stay calm. Hang on."

Maybe the man would make it after all. He had seen soldiers survive the worst kinds of wounds. He thought of a messmate, a camp favorite, a humorous, homely little fellow who had his eyes blown out and lost both legs in battle. He had dictated a cheerful letter to Buck from his hospital bed in Washington.

> The president cum in to spend sum time and crack sum jokes with me. He thanked me for what I done and I sed he was welcum. Its a good thing I cant see what a mess Im in else I mite not beleeve I am as handsum as I ever wuz, with all the hometown gals in luv with me.

Then there were others, big and strong and healthy lads who died of chills or fever or measles, or little scratches that turned ugly.

He could live if only he had water. He thought of Spangler's Spring, somewhere nearby, water that was pure and sweet and stinging cold. A gassy stench was thick around him. Dead men lay blackening in the sun, their clothes bursting from their bodies as they swelled. He did not want to look like that, or smell like that.

"Save me," begged the soldier beside him. "Oh, God . . . dear God. . . ." His voice was growing weaker. "Listen to me, God . . . please save me."

Once Buck had believed that God listened to his prayers, but that was when he was young, when Get-

169

tysburg had been a sweet, safe place to be. Now he wasn't sure. Sometimes he thought that God stayed aloof, indifferent to both hope and horror; sometimes he wondered if he prayed to something that might not even exist. What was he doing here? Did his being here, dying here, have any meaning, make any difference, accomplish any good? Who could answer him? How would he ever know the truth? Buck's lips moved silently, out of habit, in an urgent plea. *Let me live. Please, let me live.*

There was another sound drifting across the fields of suffering men. A band was playing nearby, and Buck recognized the tender melody of "Home Sweet Home."

An erect, composed figure rode slowly out of Spangler's Woods, trousers tucked neatly into bright Wellington boots, emotions tightly buttoned inside the worn, neat jacket embroidered with three stars. "It's all right . . . it's all right . . . you did your best. . . ." General Lee spoke quietly and reassuringly to the gaunt, bloodied men who seeped up from the valley, glancing at him shyly with eyes dark with misery. "You did all that men could do. It will come out all right."

Pickett reported, hurt and tearful, his long curls hanging listlessly upon his shoulders. The division was *gone,* he said in disbelief, Armistead down, Garnett and Kemper dead.

Quietly Lee told him, "This is all my fault." To another shaken officer he said, "I have lost this fight.

170

Now you must help me out of it the best way you can."

No time for remorse or analysis. Soon Meade would send a countercharge, hoping to deliver a deathblow to the weakened troops, and he must be ready for it when it came.

On his way to headquarters, the general looked out across the wrecked landscape. How familiar it all was; haversacks, knapsacks, belts and scabbards, shattered caissons, limber boxes, torn Bibles, letters, daguerreotypes, cups and combs, ruined jackets, blankets, shirts, canteens, cartridge boxes — useful implements now useless artifacts. Yet all of these could be replaced. It was the human litter scattered like rubbish across the smoking valley that made him sick with regret. Believing in himself and in them, he had sent thousands toward that distant slope, but this time he had been wrong, and those devoted men could never be recovered. The struggle would go on.

It was very hot. It was very difficult to breathe.

In the little house where he had set up his headquarters, the officers kept themselves discreetly apart. Only Walter Taylor, watchful and attentive, hovered as usual. "It's going to rain.... I can feel it in the air."

Lee said, "Yes, I can smell it coming, too." His voice was very tired.

"Strange, isn't it, sir? I mean, the way it usually storms after the big battles. It's scientific, I suppose.... The atmosphere must become disturbed by the gunfire."

"No doubt." Yet the general did not look convinced. "Or maybe it's something spiritual, Taylor. Perhaps God sends rain as a cleansing agent . . . to wash away the stains. The ugly stains. . . ." He spoke softly, absorbed in his fancy. "Yes, I think it could be that."

His aide asked, "Will you eat something now?"

"Not yet, thanks. Just leave me for a little while, would you, Taylor? I need to think. Failure is new to this camp. I must plan for it now."

Time had passed. Perhaps Meade would not press his luck after all, would not attack, would wait and see what would develop. Then let *those people* wait. There was plenty of work to be done, and quickly.

It was later, much later when the old man let his misery overflow. Dropping his face in his hands he murmured, "Too bad . . . too bad . . . oh, too bad!"

July 4

22

LEANDER CAME INTO BEKAH'S ROOM AND WAKENED her soon after midnight. There was a big commotion going on outside, he told her. Something strange was happening.

They stood at the open parlor window, straining to see what it was. Officers with lanterns were passing back and forth, talking quietly to the soldiers bivouacked in front of the houses along the street. There was the sound of horses moving and wagons bumping off into the darkness.

"The rebs are leaving," Leander whispered. "Maybe this time for good."

Bekah thought of Custis. He had promised to come back, and she was sure that he would keep his promise. She went back to bed.

Later she wakened again, this time to the sound of fife and drum. Pulling a wrapper on over her nightdress, she lit a lamp and went to the top of the stairs. A voice called from Buck's room. "Bekah?"

Adam Waite was sitting up in bed. "What's going on?"

"It's 'Yankee Doodle,' Captain!"

175

"I thought that's what it was. Help me, please. . . . I want to see."

She helped him from the bed and supported him as he walked slowly toward the window. The fresh smell of rain blew into the room through the broken panes. Below they saw a dark procession winding through a misty dawn, a flag held high.

"Those are our men!" Bekah cried. "That's our flag!"

"Then it's our fight!" Happily, awkwardly, the captain's arm tightened around her shoulders. "We've won, Bekah! Thank God it's over!"

He was a tall man, and muscular, but she felt the trembling weakness shivering through his body.

"It's the Fourth of July," he said.

"And it's my sixteenth birthday," she remembered.

A Union soldier pounded on the door in the early afternoon. Rain beat down heavily upon his head and shoulders, and dripped steadily from the peak of his forage cap. "I'm looking for . . ." he glanced at a damp envelope that he held in his hand, "Miss Rebekah Summerhill."

"Come in, please. I'm Bekah."

"No, miss. I have a report to make in town. But your house was on my way, and I thought you'd want to have this."

He had a rough, round, friendly face. "I've been on burial detail this morning at Culp's Hill. . . ." He was stammering now, anxious to finish. "And I came across one of those poor fellows, and this letter was in

176

his pocket." He held it toward her. "Well, as you can see, miss . . . it's for you."

"Burial detail?" She did not touch the envelope. She looked down, and saw his thick wet boots standing in a puddle of water on the doorstep. Then she looked up into his kind, slow-blinking eyes. "My cousin was at Culp's Hill, but he's coming back to see me. . . . I've been waiting for him."

The soldier glanced away, then back at her. "The rebels left us lots of work to do. We're digging trenches to bury the dead they left behind. . . . You see, that way we can bury forty or fifty at a time." His words stumbled off, then stopped. He tapped her arm gently with the letter, asking her to take it.

Slowly her fingers closed around it. "You're telling me that my cousin is dead."

"I'm sorry, miss."

"Are you going back up there?"

"As soon as I make my report."

"Then I want to go with you."

"Oh, I couldn't let you do that." He backed away. "It's not a sight you'd want to see, not a pretty young lady like you. No, miss, I couldn't take you there."

"Then I'll go alone."

"They won't let you up there today. It's no use trying."

She looked at him, her mind elsewhere, busy, planning, trying to slide away from what he had just told her. "I have some clothes that I can wear, and nobody will even notice me in all this rain. Just tell me where to find my cousin, please."

He hesitated, and then gave in. "Wait for me here. I'll be back soon, and I'll take you with me."

She was ready when he came, wearing Adam Waite's torn and bloodstained jacket and his trousers, held up with a belt. Her hair was piled up under his officer's hat, and she wore tall boots stuffed with rags in the toes to help make them fit.

"You shouldn't do this," the soldier said. "Really, you shouldn't."

"I have to know where Custis is." Bekah's face was cold and determined. "You're not responsible for me. Just lead the way and I'll follow."

Overhead dark clouds dragged low above the rooftops. Rain spewed from eaves, rushed and gurgled noisily in the street as men in uniform pushed past in both directions, paying no attention as she dodged through the clutter of bodies, spilled wreckage, sodden coats and caps, dead horses, and abandoned wagons. Then she was climbing over a barricade, and splashing out along the muddy pike. In minutes she was soaked through, the big hat flapping down around her ears, water leaking down her back, the too-large boots sloshing painfully at her heels.

The blurred, rounded mass of Culp's Hill rose ahead through the downpour. Picnics, and childish games, and Custis running, climbing, pulling her up the grassy slope. He'd had a way of finding tiny, hidden things, the smallest bird's egg that a breath might crush, the jewelled glitter of a ladybug, a wildflower crouched beneath a leaf. She remembered the bright blue flicker of his eyes. This was all a mistake.

Custis was not dead. He was the most alive, the most life-loving person that she knew.

Now they were climbing. She hugged her body with both arms to stop the trembling.

"Are you all right?" the soldier asked, waiting for her to catch up.

She nodded. "It looks as if the world ends here," she said.

Trees, riddled white by thousands of minie balls, were peeled naked poles stuck like spears into the dead flank of the hill. Branches dangled, were littered everywhere. She would not look at the soaked, dull-blue and earth-colored bundles that lay heaped across the melting ground.

There was the sharp scrape of metal. Men were striking at dirt with shovels, bending, scooping, heaving. A row of bodies lay nearby, the upturned faces washed clean in the rain.

At the top of the hill the soldier stopped and gestured. Beneath a shattered clump of pines was a long fresh mound, the raw, wet earth spaded over. "He's here, miss . . . at the end. I buried him myself. He was the last one in."

This was the truth of war. Death. All the words and the speeches and the sentimental songs meant nothing to her now; only this was real. Custis was dead. She believed it. She had seen war face to face, heard it, smelled it, tasted its bitter smoke. Now she touched it, bending to pick up a broken branch, wrapping it with her handkerchief. Carefully she marked the place where Custis Walker lay.

"Thank you." She held out her hand, gripped the soldier's fingers with her own. "I won't forget your kindness. Thank you."

He watched her go back down the streaming hillside, an awkward, shapeless figure in the too-large boots, dignified by grief.

My dearest Bekah:

In a little while we are going up the hill, and if I come down again there'll be no need to send this letter. If I don't come back then maybe it will find its way to you.

Bekah, I never saw anyone as lovely as you looked last night. You're not a girl at all, but a grown woman now, and I feel as if I'd lost something and found something both at the same time. Do you remember the night that you and Buck and I crawled out the cellar window and the three of us went up on Little Round Top in the moonlight? You knew that your folks would have had a holy fit if they had found out, but once you made up your mind to go, there was no stopping you. And we lay there curled up in our blankets talking for hours, and I recall how small I felt with those millions of stars shining over our heads, and I said we were only tiny parts of something too big to believe, and you said yes, but VERY IMPORTANT parts all the same. I liked that. You have always been a VERY IMPORTANT part of my life.

That night on Round Top when you fell asleep, I stayed awake and watched over you, and it was the very best time of my life, until last night when I was kissing you.

Your own,
Custis

180

23

BUCK HAD PRAYED FOR WATER TO COOL THE FEVER
and quench his terrible thirst, and then it came at
last, a fine misty drizzle at the start, then cold nee-
dling strokes, and then the deluge that punched
across parched acres, soaking deep into the ground,
brimming in the hollows, filling dry creek beds to
overflowing. Helpless men, trapped in the low-lying
places, cried out to be moved, terrified of drown-
ing.

"Buck! Buck Summerhill! Summerhill . . . Summerhill . . . Summerhill. . . ." It was his own name,
tumbling over and over in his mind. Sometimes it
sounded louder and nearer, and then it floated off
and disappeared.

He had tried to get up, to crawl to some protected
spot, but he was too weak from hunger and loss of
blood. His corner of the field was heaped with soldiers, most of them silent now, oblivious. No warmth
or comfort here; he was alone, soaked through and
violently shaking, chilled to the heart.

"Buck! Buck Summerhill!"

"Here." The word was too small, barely a whisper.
He tried again. "Here I am . . . over here. . . ." But his
voice was washed away in windy gusts of water that

lashed in waves across the fields. He listened. Thunder banged heavily overhead, but he did not hear his name called again.

Then he was in the house on Baltimore Street, going up the stairs, his legs almost too tired to move. He went into his room, and with a great effort climbed up onto the bed. Quilts fluttered over him, surrounded him. He was warm and safe in his own place, and at last he could sleep. He felt the deep, soft feather mattress sink beneath him, taking him down and down.

"Buck!"

He did not want to open his eyes. Someone was shaking him, forcing him to stay awake. An arm slipped around his upper body and lifted him. "Buck! Come on, Buck!"

A face stared down at him.

"Come on, Buck," Tully said. "We're going home."

Others were also going home. Throughout the long, dark, sullen afternoon, through the steady hiss and military rattle of the rain, Lee had waited to see what the Union commander would do. By nightfall he knew there would be no attack. It was then he pulled his troops off the ridge and started the long procession homeward through the mountain passes; soldiers, wagons, prisoners, jolting ambulances, seventeen miles of misery retreating through mud and storms toward Virginia.

* * *

Meade sent a joyful message to the President. The result of the battle was glorious, the enemy utterly baffled and defeated. He would look to the army for greater efforts *to drive from our soil every vestige of the presence of the invader.*

Those words annoyed and offended a deeply worried Abraham Lincoln. Driving the enemy away was not the way to end the conflict. It would only prolong it. The rebel forces must be destroyed before the war could be ended and the great issues settled. Time and time again Lincoln had tried to persuade the military minds to see it his way. Yet no one, except perhaps the stubborn general who had besieged Vicksburg and won it on the same day that the Gettysburg battle had ended, had been able to grasp what was so simple and so obvious to the burdened President.

General Meade must go after Lee and smash the Army of Northern Virginia.

But the Union commander was slow to react. His losses, twenty-three thousand dead, wounded, or missing, were enormous. How could soldiers who had given so much be asked to give even more? And even though the limping Southern army must have suffered just as much, it would always be dangerous. After a cautious interval the general stalked the enemy warily, putting his troops between the Confederates and Washington, but taking no foolish chances. Days later, when Meade had finally decided it was time to strike, Lee, who was one jump ahead, leaped the Potomac with his men and escaped.

* * *

The town swelled, groaning with casualties. Churches, schools, private houses, barns, outbuildings, stores and warehouses, Gettysburg College, and the Seminary building were jammed with patients, and still they kept coming in from the battlefield, badly shattered men needing medical treatment, food and shelter, and a kindly human touch.

"You can't go back to the hospital without some rest." Bekah was worried about her mother, who was spending most of her time with the wounded soldiers. "Dr. Horner told me you were to stay quiet." She did not mention the nerves. Mrs. Summerhill seemed to have forgotten all about them, and Bekah hoped that they had gone for good.

"I need to be there." Lydia Summerhill was dressed to go out. "And every time a man is brought in I look to make sure it isn't Buck or Tully or one of your cousins."

Bekah hadn't told her mother yet about Custis. She had put the knowledge of his death away on a dark shelf in her mind. Later there would be time for them to mourn, to take him to the family plot on Cemetery Hill. She was sure that would be what Aunt Mercy would want them to do.

"It's odd how many of the Southern boys remark how they can't believe how people here in Gettysburg treat them just as we do our own," her mother said. "But of course we do! When someone is hurting he isn't blue or gray or any color at all, he's one of the family, isn't that so?"

"Yes." It was so. Already the house was full of the

injured from both armies. Caring for them would take all of their energy. There was no room here for hate.

"The Montforts went to the railroad station to help," Mrs. Summerhill said, "and young Mary Elizabeth found her own father lying there with a hole in his side. He'd been hit by a shell. Well, her mother told her to go home quick and take care of her grandma and her sister, but Mary Elizabeth knew that he was dying. What an awful shock for the poor little thing."

Leander came into the kitchen, his arms heaped with old bed linen to be used for bandages. "The rebs killed Owen Robinson's pigs. Charles feels bad about it, but they didn't find his slingshot."

"They didn't find the cow hidden in the parlor, either," Bekah said. "But the way this town's been shaking, the Snyders will be getting butter from her now instead of milk."

Leander didn't even smile. "Today is the Fourth of July," he said sadly, "and just a few days ago Charles and I were wishing we could make some noise to celebrate."

"I think we've had all the noise we can stand," said his mother. "We'll do our celebrating some other time."

"I don't even care about it. It doesn't matter any more."

"Oh, Rebekah!" Mrs. Summerhill put her arms around her daughter and hugged her. "It's your birthday!"

"That doesn't seem important either," Bekah told her. "But I know it's a day that I'll never forget."

She helped carry the linen down the hall and opened the door. The street was filled with Union soldiers. Two men walked slowly toward the house, the taller man supporting the other, a soldier with his leg cut off at the knee.

"So many . . . too many," her mother whispered. "It breaks my heart to see these youngsters maimed like that, crippled for life."

Bekah still couldn't see the faces clearly, and yet something about the soldiers held her attention, kept her there, staring at them. Then she knew.

"It's Buck! That's Tully helping him!" She ran toward them. "Buck, you're home! Thank God, you're home!"

Standing on the doorstep, Mrs. Summerhill began to cry.

After

24

November 19, 1863

IT WAS A DAY IN LATE NOVEMBER, A DAY ALIVE WITH sunshine, the sky a clean and vivid blue. There was a snap and clarity to the air that reminded Bekah, wrapped in a warm woolen shawl, that winter would soon huddle down from the north.

"I wish it would snow." She moved with the crowd strolling out along the Baltimore turnpike. Buck, still unaccustomed to his wooden leg, swung awkwardly ahead, apart from the rest of them, just out of reach of her voice. Bekah hurried to catch up with him. "I wish it would snow for days and days and cover up the streets and houses and everything ... out there ... until it was all hard and white and frozen stiff. So it would look as if nothing had happened here, nothing at all."

"Something did happen." Sometimes Buck spoke so softly it was hard to understand him. "Snow won't change anything. Nothing will be the same here again. Don't you know that?"

He was right. She did know it. The war had come and rolled over them and rumbled away, leaving Gettysburg a different place than it had been before. Even the people had changed. Everyone seemed older. Sadder, too. Maybe that was what she had wanted, the blankness and purity of fresh snow to whiten the dark sadness of the town.

"So many have come," said Mrs. Summerhill, impressed by the size of the crowd. "And imagine someone as famous as Mr. Everett coming here to speak to us at the dedication ceremony."

"I hate long, boring speeches," Bekah said. "I only came to see President Lincoln."

"I've already seen him." Leander, walking behind with Charles McCurdy, kept bumping into his sister, sending her hoop skirts swinging. "He came out of Mr. Wills's house last night at the Diamond, when everyone was calling for him, but I couldn't hear what he said."

"He said, 'Go home, little boy. It's past your bedtime,' " Bekah teased.

"He did *not!* But he had this funny high voice." Leander made a squeaky noise in his throat.

"I heard him. He was nice. He smiled and was friendly, but he didn't have a speech to make just then." Charles was a good mimic. He stretched himself taller, hollowed his cheeks, stroked an imaginary beard. "He said, 'In my position it is sometimes important that I should not say foolish things,' and the man behind me yelled, 'If you can help it!' "

"That was very unkind," said Mrs. Summerhill. It

upset her when people said cruel things about Abraham Lincoln, or printed them in the newspapers. "I'm surprised he even found the time to travel with so much on his mind. And to think the committee didn't even give him a special invitation at first. It was only when they knew he planned on being here that they invited him to say a few words. But then, I don't suppose anyone ever thought he would come, a busy man like that with all his worries." She looked around her at the men, women, and children streaming along the road. "Or so many thousands of people."

"And so many soldiers." It was all the men in uniform that surprised Bekah, men on crutches or with empty coat sleeves pinned up, or, like Buck, hobbling along on artificial legs. "Why would they want to come back and be reminded?"

"Maybe they need to know what happened here, and why," Buck said.

"Don't they already know?" she asked him.

"I used to think I knew." His voice was so low that Bekah leaned closer to catch his words. "Now I wonder. I wonder about a lot of things these days."

She had been close to her brother once, but that had changed, too, ever since he had come home from the battle. Being friends with him seemed long ago, in another time. So much had happened since. Soon after General Lee had retreated, the Union army had gone away, too, taking surgeons and medical attendants with it, and leaving thousands of casualties in Gettysburg. Quickly the town had filled with people, anxious mothers and fathers and wives and children, all worried and searching. The Sanitary and Christian Commissions had arrived with supplies and support; hospital tents had been set up and staffed; and for many weeks all the public buildings and private homes had been filled with the wounded and with the relatives who came to visit them. Buzzards came too, ugly and sinister birds that circled slowly in the sky before they dropped to devour what they could scavenge. For weeks a taint of decay hovered over the county, and not even chloride of lime, thickly scattered, could cover the sickening odor.

There were flies, millions of them, and illness caused by pestilence. Citizens died from it. Strangers kept arriving, more and more every day, wanting to wade through the great, dead valley in search of mementos, as if they hoped to make their own lives bigger and more important by carrying away a piece of what had happened in the fields of Gettysburg.

Tully had gone back to Erie to be with his folks. Buck had gone to see him, but when he came back all he would say was that a part of Tully Willard was still missing, and he was not sure his friend would ever be completely whole again.

Captain Waite had recovered and gone home to Batavia to marry his sweetheart. He had written a warm note to thank the Summerhills, but he had not mentioned his wedding, and Bekah didn't want to know about it, anyway. She had the feeling that Anna would trouble the man for the rest of his life.

Now there was a disturbance going on along the

road, guns firing in the distance, and the quick, bright thump of a marching band. People were stopping, pressing back against the broken fences, unmended since the days of the battle.

"It's the parade! Here it comes!" Charles shouted.

Columns of soldiers passed by in a blur of crashing brass and strident trumpets and the booming blows of a big bass drum.

"Look!" Leander was hopping up and down. "Look who's coming!"

Buck barely noticed the important flanking officials. His attention was focused on a striking figure on horseback. It was a worn-looking man with deep-set, shadowed eyes, bony wrists sticking out from the sleeves of a Prince Albert coat, long legs almost dragging on the ground. He was not like other politicians Buck had seen, riding the adulation of a cheering crowd. This one slumped forward, swaying through a melancholy landscape of his own, unaware of all the curious faces staring at him. Stark. Isolated. Lonely. It was as if some hidden grief within him weighed him down. *That's how I feel*, Buck thought. *He looks the way I feel inside.*

Voices called out, "Mr. President! On to Richmond, Mr. President! We're with you all the way!" There were more enthusiastic cheers, and the warm rustle of clapping hands.

Abraham Lincoln returned from the distant place where he had been. Lifted an arm. A smile touched the corner of his lips as he nodded at the spectators, touching them with his keen and friendly glance. His eyes met Buck's with kindness, and his smile deepened at the sight of Mrs. McClellan's five-month-old baby, heavily bundled and furiously roaring, held up for him to admire. Buck often thought of Jennie Wade who had never known that her sweetheart, Jack, had died soon after he was wounded at Winchester.

The President passed out of sight.

Farther along a high rise of land gave a sweeping view of the battlefield. Here, close to the place where the Louisiana Tigers had been thrown back on the night of July 2, a seventeen-acre site had been set aside for a national cemetery to honor the dead. Crews had been busy for weeks digging graves in a semicircle, burying soldiers by states, with a small and simple headstone for each man. A place had also been designated for a permanent monument to be raised later. A low wooden platform, draped with bunting, had been erected for the dedication ceremony.

By the time the Summerhills reached the area there was a vast, shifting, murmuring mass of fifteen thousand people. Buck disappeared among the crowd, and minutes later Bekah saw that he had worked his way up to the front of the platform. The stage was filled with officials, military men, cabinet members, and state governors. The President was seated on a low settee, with Secretary of State Seward on his left, and an empty space was reserved for the famous guest speaker, who had not yet arrived.

Bekah caught a glimpse of Tillie Pierce among the

spectators. Something had finally happened to Tillie. During the battle, when she had been trapped on the Weikert farm out near the Round Tops, she had carried water to the wounded men and talked to General Weed in the cellar of the house just before he died. One day, she said, she would write it all down. Beside her, ribbons bouncing with excitement, was the little Montfort girl. It was Mary Elizabeth, who had found her own father dying at the railroad station. There were hundreds of stories; everyone in Gettysburg had one to tell. Bekah thought that perhaps someday she would write about those vivid days herself.

Eleven o'clock. Eleven fifteen. Eleven thirty. The ceremony was half an hour late, and word passed that Mr. Everett was still touring the battlefield, preparing his address.

"The idea," fussed Mrs. Summerhill. "Keeping the President waiting!" Onstage, officials whispered among themselves, and went away, and hurried back. Only Mr. Lincoln seemed composed and good-tempered as he looked out into the restless crowd. Men and women fidgeted, stamping their feet and rubbing their chilled hands to keep warm. Hungry babies were jiggled up and down. It was now eleven forty-five.

Mrs. Summerhill's cheeks flamed with cold, and her nose burned, a red, indignant dot. "I can't imagine who this Mr. Everett thinks he is," she fumed. "Famous or not, he's being downright disrespectful!"

Shortly before twelve Leander ran up. "Mr. Burns says he's been invited to meet Abraham Lincoln later on! And he's been bragging about all the things he's going to tell him about fighting in the battle, and Mrs. Burns says it's a pity that only his head has grown so big, and not the rest of him!"

Bekah laughed. Then she saw someone. "Mother . . . over there . . . near Mrs. McCurdy. . . ."

"Who is it?"

"Isn't that Captain Waite?"

Mrs. Summerhill, nearsighted from her needle-work, squinted into the distance, and then shook her head. "He looks familiar, but I couldn't say for sure."

"I'm going to go and see."

It took some time to get there. Pushing, wriggling in and out of the crowd, Bekah finally reached a tall bearded man in a cavalry uniform, standing with his arms folded across his broad chest. When she did reach his side she felt suddenly shy and unsure of herself. "Captain Waite?"

There was no doubt that he recognized her, or that he was very pleased to see her. "Bekah! Bekah Summerhill!"

"I thought it was you," she told him. "I'm happy to see you looking so well."

"I'm very well, thanks to you good people. In fact, I'll be reporting back for duty in a week or so." He smiled down at her. "I planned to pay a call on you after the ceremony."

"Then you must stay to dinner with us."

"You did get my letter, the one that I wrote from Batavia?"

She nodded.

"I had hoped you would write to me, Bekah ... keep in touch."

She didn't know what to tell him. How confused and difficult those long days had been during the summer and into the fall when everyone in town had set aside their own lives to care for the casualties. The Summerhills had had men in the house until the end of October, and the last wounded soldier had left Gettysburg only a few days ago. There had been so many things to do, so many details to attend to. They had buried Custis in the family plot in the Evergreen Cemetery, among the rows of broken tombstones that had been smashed during the battle. She had written his epitaph herself: *At rest in the far land of peace.* It still hurt to go there, to put wildflowers on his grave, to think of him. They had heard from Mason, who was in a Northern prison on Johnson's Island in Lake Erie, and they had sent him parcels full of nourishing food, hoping to keep him alive.

"Your friend, Anna," she said. "She must be pleased to have had you at home all these months."

"Anna married while I was away. I was surprised ... and hurt ... but that's all over now."

"I'm sorry." Bekah was indignant that the woman had mistreated this decent man. "And you're going back into the army? Do you think the war will last much longer, Captain?"

"Yes, it probably will. General Grant is going to wear out Lee's men, and grind down the South, no matter how long it takes. And I believe it will cost us all a great deal, but there seems to be no other way."

There was, at last, a motion of beginning on the platform. Bekah saw that a dignified man with long, white hair and a confident face had taken his place beside the President.

"I'd better get back to my mother now."

"No, stay with me, Bekah. I need you here." Smiling, he put out his hands, cupping them around the red blaze of her hair, pretending to warm them. "And if the crowd gets really restless, you can entertain us with twenty or thirty choruses of 'The Union Forever.'"

"You remember that first day I saw you?"

"I remember every day with you."

Two hours later Edward Everett was still speaking, but Bekah, who had lost all track of time, would not have noticed if he had talked away the afternoon.

Buck had taken a place directly in front of the platform. He had stood there, chilly and uncomfortable, as the orator spoke to the attentive crowd in silvery phrases that soared and dazzled, melting off into the sparkling autumn air. Buck listened carefully. The words told him about a battle that had occurred in the fields and woods of Gettysburg, but they didn't tell him what it had meant, or why it had mattered. For a long time he had felt that his manhood, with all its warm strong feelings, had crumbled away, that his heart and bones and blood were dry as dust. He still felt that way. He wondered why he had come.

Applause lifted and sank and lifted higher in thick approving waves. Gleaming with success, Mr. Everett sat down. The Baltimore Glee Club sang an anthem specially written for the dedication. Quickly the President of the United States was introduced to make a few final remarks.

The tall, dark man stood up and stepped forward. He spoke quietly and briefly, for two or three minutes, and when he had finished a polite scattered response rippled out through the crowd. It had been a long, tiring ceremony, and everyone was ready to go home. Voices rose majestically as the choir sang "O! It is Sweet for our Country to Die!," and it was over. Officials bobbed busily about the platform, shaking hands, talking enthusiastically as people streamed away into the bright November sunlight, eager to get home to warm houses and hot dinners.

Buck stood, unable to move, his eyes on the brooding face of the man who had just spoken. For months he had asked himself hard questions about the great thing he had been a part of. The struggle he had once believed in had become a puzzle to him, had seemed at times a tragic waste. Now, in simple and direct and truthful words, this sad-eyed man had given him its meaning. The battle fought during those hot days in July had mattered, and every life lost here had mattered, too. On these slopes of war men had paid in blood and sacrifice so that the bright winged spirit of the nation could be kept alive, and the beautiful word, *freedom,* passed on as a gift to all the generations that would follow.

He knew by his look of disappointment that the tall man realized that what he had just said had not been grasped or understood or believed. Buck wished he could reassure him in some way that the little speech, so large with meaning, had not been a failure. The concept of liberty would always baffle and elude and challenge the human mind, but what Abraham Lincoln had said was something that he would remember for the rest of his life.

The President came down the wooden steps. The little Montfort girl, bright-faced and expectant, smiled up at him.

"Hello, young lady. Who are you?"

"I'm Mary Elizabeth."

He bent, scooped up her tiny hand. For the second time that day, his eyes met Buck's.

"Thank you," the boy said. "Thank you, Mr. President." Then he turned and moved away, a lonely figure limping off among the thinning crowd.

What Was Said

Four score and seven years ago our fathers brought forth on this continent, a new nation, conceived in Liberty, and dedicated to the proposition that all men are created equal.

Now we are engaged in a great civil war; testing whether that nation, or any nation so conceived and so dedicated, can long endure. We are met on a great battlefield of that war. We have come to dedicate a portion of that field as a final resting-place for those who here gave their lives that that nation might live. It is altogether fitting and proper that we should do this.

But, in a larger sense, we cannot dedicate — we cannot consecrate — we cannot hallow — this ground. The brave men, living and dead, who struggled here have consecrated it, far above our poor power to add or detract. The world will little note, nor long remember, what we say here, but it can never forget what they did here. It is for us the living, rather, to be dedicated here to the unfinished work which they who fought here have thus far so nobly advanced. It is rather for us to be here dedicated to the great task remaining before us — that from these honored dead we take increased devotion to that cause for which they gave the last full measure of devotion; that we here highly resolve that these dead shall not have died in vain; that this nation, under God, shall have a new birth of freedom; and that government of the people, by the people, for the people, shall not perish from the earth.